DEPRAVED ROYALS

A DARK RUSSIAN MAFIA ROMANCE

CARA BIANCHI

Copyright © 2022 - Cara Bianchi

Cover © 2022 - @covers_by_wonderland (Instagram)

All rights reserved.

No part of this book may be reproduced in any form or by any electronic or mechanical means, including information storage and retrieval systems, without written permission from the author, except for the use of brief quotations in a book review.

TRIGGER WARNINGS

It's my responsibility as an author to be clear about any possible triggers in the book. Your safety and mental health are very important, so please don't read this story if you may be adversely affected by the following:

- **public sex**

- **BDSM**

- **sexual violence (brief)**

- **references to child abuse (physical and emotional)**

- **plot-contextual violence**

- **pregnancy loss**

- **depictions of narcissism, psychosis and suicidal ideation**

- **abusive family dynamics**

MAILING LIST

Get a FREE BONUS CHAPTER by signing up to my mailing list!

Sign up at this link:

https://dl.bookfunnel.com/n5celyg56k

CONTENTS

1.	Dani	1
2.	Kal	10
3.	Dani	20
4.	Dani	29
5.	Kal	36
6.	Dani	44
7.	Dani	50
8.	Kal	56
9.	Kal	64
10.	Dani	70
11.	Dani	77
12.	Kal	83
13.	Kal	91
14.	Dani	101
15.	Kal	112
16.	Dani	119
17.	Dani	131
18.	Kal	139
19.	Dani	148
20.	Kal	156
21.	Dani	165
22.	Kal	172
23.	Dani	179
24.	Kal	187
25.	Dani	193
26.	Dani	201
27.	Kal	211
28.	Dani	217
29.	Kal	225
30.	Kal	232
	Epilogue	239
	Epilogue	254

Mailing List 265
Also by Cara Bianchi 267

1
DANI

When the man with the ice-blue eyes looks my way, how could I help but notice him?

The airport is crammed with people, all shouting and stressing out about the snow piling up outside. Departures are dropping off the board with every passing minute. Everyone is furious except him.

He's an oasis of serenity in the middle of it all, lying across a bench in the waiting area next to the gate, oblivious to the tuts and grumbles of those who resent his seat-hogging.

I haven't got time to focus on him. I need to run. I have to get back to New York by tomorrow, or my parents will kill me. I'm stuck here in Geneva if I don't make my flight. And I'm already late.

The sound of my stupidly loud heels thudding on the floor is what gets his attention. He sits up in time to meet my eyes, and all of a sudden, all I want to do is stop and stare at him.

He's fucking *beautiful*. How he's not surrounded by people just gawping slack-jawed at his hotness is beyond me. Despite my hurry, I slow down and hold his gaze for a beat as I pass...

The tannoy system crackles, a nasal-sounding voice booming out.

"Last call for Danica Pushkin. That's Danica Pushkin, gate twelve. Boarding is about to close."

Shit.

I find another gear and pick up speed, weaving through the throng as I near the gate. Something compels me to look over my shoulder, and my blood runs cold.

The sexy man is there. He isn't even working hard to keep up. He strides purposefully, and the crowd parts, cutting a path directly to me.

It's not as though he's done anything. He only looked at me. There's no law against it.

But I'm scared.

I need to get to the gate. I can't miss this flight. Almost there...

I feel a wrenching pain in my shoulder, and I'm pulled backward. The sudden change of direction unbalances me, and I hit the ground hard.

I look to see a thin man with a scruff of patchy beard and a dirty army surplus jacket. He's pulling at my purse, dragging the strap off my arm.

"Get the fuck off me!" I cry, wrapping my arm around the strap and yanking it hard. The man responds by kicking me firmly in the ribcage, and the pain is enough to bring tears to my eyes.

The back of my head smashes on the floor. I can see the bright lights overhead, but for a few seconds, nothing else is registering.

Then I hear him.

"You fucking sneaky *truslivyy* cunt."

I know that word, of course. It means 'coward.'

I scramble to my feet to find the hot guy sitting on top of my attacker, his knee wedged into the man's throat.

I look around, but no one is paying attention. The security officers are so nonchalant that they may as well be watching a ballet or something. I wave my hands, trying to get them to notice what's happening.

"What the hell? Hey! Aren't you gonna —"

A squeal from the man on the ground cuts my voice off. I look just in time to see the hot guy deliver a firm punch to his jaw, whipping the man's head to one side. Blood spatters across the polished floor.

My purse is still in my attacker's hand.

Crack. Another punch splinters his nose, and he howls pitifully.

He doesn't let go of my purse, and there's no way I'm going over there to get it.

I pat my coat, feeling the outline of my boarding card and passport tucked safely in my inside pocket. Like my father always told me - you can't be too careful.

I turn away from the fight and run, hoping I'm not too late.

My shoes squeal on the floor as I take a corner fast, sprinting for the gate. A steward is putting a small sign on the desk just as I crash into it, slapping my passport on the counter.

"I'm here," I gasp. "It's me. I'm Danica Pushkin. Ready to board."

The steward cocks his head and gives me a condescending half-smile. "I'm so sorry, ma'am. The flight is departing now. You're too late."

I look over his shoulder to see the Boeing, barely visible through the blizzard. It's already moving, taxiing towards the runway.

I look back at the steward and give him my best ditzy expression. With me being only twenty, it's often possible to give the impression that I'm a massive idiot who knows nothing about the world. If I can get this guy to take pity on me, maybe he can call the plane back...

"So here's the thing," I begin. "I need —"

"A ride?"

I turn around, furious at being cut off mid-sentence, to see those cold blue eyes again.

How is he here, standing behind me like nothing happened?

"What?" I say.

"You need a ride," he replies. His mouth tilts into a devilish grin, and I suddenly feel restless and warm inside.

Oh, for fuck's sake, Dani. He's attractive. Very attractive. So what?

Well, it'd help if he didn't use such a provocative turn of phrase. Because *fuck* yes, I'd like a ride very much indeed.

I turn away from the sexy smile and back to the desk jockey. "This is my flight," I say, waving my boarding card at the steward, "and I have paid for it. If you can't recall it, I want to be booked onto another one immediately, please."

I hear a derisive snort of laughter from behind me, but I ignore it. The steward raises his eyebrows.

"There are no more flights to New York today, I'm afraid."

I'm about to lose my shit when the hottie reaches past me and picks up my passport.

"I'll deal with her," he says to the steward. He turns, my passport in his hand, and starts walking away.

For a moment, I'm lost for a reaction. I stare at his retreating back for a few seconds before turning to remonstrate with the steward again. He's walking away too.

I look from one man to the other and make my choice.

"Hey!" I shout. "You, Mr. I'll Deal With Her? Who the *fuck* do you think you are?"

He stops and turns around to look at me. He extends a hand as though we're meeting at a conference.

"I'm Kal," he says. "And you are... let me guess." I slap his hand away, and he grins. "I got it. Furious, right?"

"What is your problem?" I ask. "I had it under control. That guy was going to get the plane to come back for me."

"Yep, I'm sure he was," Kal says. "Then he was going to turn water into wine, invent time travel and, just maybe, make the in-flight food taste amazing."

I narrow my eyes at him. "Oh, great. A stalker, a brawler, and a comedian too? What luck I have."

He shrugs. "So," he says, looking at the name on my passport, "Danica. Do you want to get out of Geneva or not?"

"Of course I do. How do you propose we get there? We can't fly."

"Not as far as New York, no. My arms get tired."

I close my eyes.

"You know what I mean. You heard the guy. There are no flights out of Geneva."

"There aren't any commercial flights, but I have my own plane, and if I want to take off, we take off. No one in this airport will try to stop me."

I look at him, searching his face, but I can't see anything other than his sharp jaw and supple lips as they curl into a smile once again. There's no sign that he's an actual psycho, but that's the whole point, isn't it?

Monsters come in pretty packaging.

I decide asking too many questions is a shortcut to sleeping in an airport hotel tonight...

"Oh!" I cry. "My purse! Did you get it back for me?"

Kal frowns. "No, I didn't. What I *did* was beat that fucker until he was gargling his last Will and Testament, and then my friends in security took him away. That good enough?"

I don't know how to respond. "Why were you following me?"

"What the fuck?" Kal slaps his forehead with his palm. "You have to be shitting me. Are you this naïve?"

Calling me that is like a red rag to a bull. No, I am not naïve. I come from a world where people live and die by their wits, and I know more than most about the danger of taking unnecessary risks. My father never shuts up about it.

Be careful, Dani. Remember who you are. You're a Bratva princess. You can't swan around like you're just anybody...

"Don't call me that," I hiss. "What are you talking about?"

"*I* wasn't following you," Kal says, "*he* was. When I saw you run past, he was right behind you, ready to relieve you of that Birkin purse. How dumb can you get, walking through an airport with your wealth on display like that?" He looks me up and down. "I mean, you're fucking smoking hot. Do you really *need* to do anything to attract attention to yourself?"

I'm surprised by the compliment, and I flush. He notices that I'm scrambling for a response and rescues me.

"It's alright. You can't help that you're the damsel type," he says. "I knew you were about to get in trouble and decided to help, that's all. Nothing more to it."

"You nearly killed the guy," I say. "That's quite the reaction."

Kal furrows his brow as though the thought hadn't occurred to him before.

"I guess it is," he says, "but I got rid of him either way. So you owe me."

I glare at him. "Oh, really? What do I owe you?"

He shows me the palms of his hands. "Nothing sinister. Just the pleasure of your company. You can rifle through the lost property for a thirty-thousand-dollar purse that will definitely not be there, followed by a long wait on a shit-awful metal bench. Or you can enjoy a comfortable seat on my plane." He grins. "Champagne and suede leather, or back pain and shit weather. Your choice."

I laugh. "You made a rhyme. That's kind of impressive."

Kal winks at me. "I have many things I can impress you with, *milaya*."

Oh, no. Don't be calling me 'honey.' I can't deal with it. But that being said, I desperately want to hear him say it again.

He looks into my eyes steadily. "What's it gonna be, Danica?"

"Okay," I say. "But you can call me Dani."

He offers me his arm, and I feel his taut bicep through his jacket as my hand slips over it.

He leans close to my ear.

"Great. That's a good girl."

I'd have swooned to the floor if I wasn't holding onto him. I grip his arm tightly, and he gives a quiet chuckle.

"Let's go. The plane's prepped and ready."

2

KAL

I enjoy watching her.

She's curled up on the cream leather seat, her shoes on the floor beside her. Her eyes are closed, and a small smile plays on her lips.

Dani Pushkin.

I can't believe I tripped over her just like that. Her name rang through the airport, and I looked up to see a gorgeous girl running like the hounds of hell were after her.

I don't feel bad for the guy I beat up. Dani was carrying a purse that he could sell for a small fortune. He would have probably died of an overdose once he could afford all the drugs he could ever want.

But *damn*. I couldn't believe it when I realized she had no idea the junkie was following her. She saw *me*, though. When she turned and looked over her shoulder, our eyes met, and for a second, I wondered if she could see every vicious thought I ever had about her poisonous cesspit of a family. She clearly doesn't know who I am, or she'd have run in the opposite direction until her feet were bloody.

Dani sighs in her sleep, and her lips part. My cock thickens at the sight.

I wish someone had *told* me. Surely it's not much to ask for someone to say, 'hey, you know the daughter of your family's despised nemesis? She's the most fuckable thing you'll ever see.'

But now she's on my plane, and although she doesn't know it yet, we're not going to New York.

I let myself into the cockpit. I don't know the pilot - I hire a new guy every time I fly, on a one-trip basis, to reduce the risk of getting hijacked by some asshole hired by one of my enemies. The pilot seems okay, but he's clearly not thrilled by my habit of changing plans.

"So you want us to stop at Heathrow?" he asks. "Why?"

"No reason, but you need to think of one" I reply. "Just give it a minute, then announce it. We're landing in London because of poor visibility, UFOs, or whatever the fuck you like. Clear?"

"For what you're paying me, yes, that's absolutely clear."

I return to the cabin to find Dani sitting up, rubbing her eyes with the heel of her hand.

"I can't believe I slept," she says.

I hand her a glass of champagne from the tray on the table and take my seat opposite her.

"Don't worry about it. Have a drink. You'll feel better."

Dani sips the champagne and hiccups. "Fizzy," she says. "I can't help it. I do that every time. It's lovely stuff, though."

The sun streams in through the window, making her pale skin glow. She crosses her legs, and her skirt rides up, revealing an extra inch of creamy thigh.

I will hear her scream my name before this day is through.

I don't care that she's a Pushkin. She's in dire need of a hard fuck, and I'm the man to give it to her.

She leans back in her chair, the light catching the hollow of her throat. I imagine my hand around her neck, the other gripping her hip as I fuck her pussy from behind, ideally over that chair...

I'm developing a problem.

"Excuse me," I say. "I'll be right back."

I lock myself in the bathroom cubicle and lean against the wall, closing my eyes.

I could just drag Dani in here with me. Push her to her knees and thrust my cock into her mouth until she gags. Get it good and wet so I can balance her on this tiny basin and wreck her little pink pussy until I come inside her.

My cock is too hard to ignore. I free it from my pants and jerk it for a minute to relieve the ache.

But I know how to wait. I want to take my time. Really go to work on her. I won't be satisfied until she screams herself hoarse and soaks the sheets with her pleasure.

A crackle and the pilot is speaking over the PA system. His voice is enough to kill the mood, and I zip myself up as he talks.

"So sorry, sir. Due to weather conditions, we will have to stop in England, specifically Heathrow International, London. Stand by for landing and re-take your seats, please."

I leave the bathroom and sit down again. Dani's expression is one of panic.

"London?" she says. "I don't have anywhere to go in London, and I need to get home today! It's my parent's wedding anniversary party, and I promised them I'd be there."

How sweet. Fyodor and Marta Pushkin, celebrating their happiness. I hope they fucking enjoy it because it's the last anniversary they'll ever have.

"I'm sure they'll understand," I say. I pick up a champagne flute and knock it back, wincing. "Fuck me. That's disgusting."

Dani looks on the verge of tears. She wrings her hands anxiously as she looks at me.

I know I'm a sick bastard. Her shining eyes turn me on more than they should.

Dani sits up straight and pulls herself together, throwing a big smile at me. It's adorable.

"So, I guess I have to make the best of it," she says. "I don't have money or cards, but I can sort it out, I'm sure."

"You are staying with me."

There's a long pause. I decide to keep talking before she comes up with a reason to refuse. Because her motives are of no interest to me, and I won't take them into account, there's no need to waste her time or mine debating it.

"I have a suite in Knightsbridge," I say. "It's empty as my family is in New York. You and I can stay there tonight. I'll make sure you get on the earliest possible commercial flight home tomorrow if you're still this keen to get away from me."

Dani opens her mouth to say something but decides against it.

"Well, I've come this far," she says. "Why not?"

The suite has been serviced and is spotless. It's a large, airy space with a private elevator and panoramic windows on all four sides.

Dani is loosening up a little. We've both had a decent amount of the ice-cold Russian Standard that is always in my refrigerator, and while I'm used to it, I have to assume she isn't. She's not drunk, but she's got the pleasant buzz that comes with a good vodka.

The concierge knows me well and has provided me with my usual comforts. I made an additional request, and now he's knocking at the door.

I walk back into the lounge, carrying a large suitcase.

Dani frowns. "That's not mine. My bag is probably lonely on the carousel at JFK right now."

"This," I say, "*is* yours. Got you a few clothing items, toiletries, that sort of thing. A shower and clean clothes are a basic human right."

She smiles. "Thank you, Kal."

Hearing her say my name is fucking hot. Her thanking me is even more alluring.

I wanna do things to her she'll be grateful for.

Dani lies back on the sofa.

"I feel better now, and I'll feel better still when I've had a shower." She frowns. "I probably shouldn't drink. I'm just worried about my parents."

"It's legal here. You're good." I top up my glass. "They gonna fuck you up for not getting home on time?"

She shoots me a glance, her eyes widening. "No," she says, confused. "They *love* me. I don't enjoy disappointing them." She wrinkles her nose. "Weird of you to go straight to them being assholes. What are *your* parents like?"

Nope. We aren't going there. My mother is *not* a suitable subject for conversation. She lives rent-free in my head as it is, without me talking about her too.

"They're not here." I sit beside her on the sofa. "And let's just say I'm glad of it."

Dani leans back, looking at me through half-closed eyes.

"Am I only here because you want sex?"

I set down my glass on the table.

So you wanna play? You got it.

"You think I'm that kind of guy?"

"Yep. I do." She tilts her head and smirks. "You kicked the shit out of a mugger and then took my passport from me like it was a deed of ownership. Since then, you've told me how it's gonna be."

She pulls her legs onto the sofa and stretches out so her feet almost touch me.

"So be honest. You want to fuck me, don't you?"

Fucking damn right.

I turn to her and put my hands on her knees, pulling her legs apart so I can settle my body along hers. She's warm, her skin smooth and soft. I place my hand on the back of her neck and feel her back arch, her tits pressing against my chest.

"I *am* that kind of guy," I murmur beside her ear. "And I *am* gonna fuck you, Dani, because you need it. Don't you?"

She nods, then gasps as I kiss her neck, biting gently.

"I don't know you," she says, "and I don't care. I wanted you inside me from the second I saw you."

I shift my weight, pressing my hard cock against her pussy through her skirt. My hand steals down her body, sliding her skirt until I find her panties. I slip my fingertips through the leg hole and under the fabric.

"You are soaked," I say, rubbing my fingers between her silky-smooth pussy lips. "I can't wait to get in here."

"Then *don't* wait," she says, her voice taking on an urgent edge. I catch her swollen clit with my index finger, and she hisses through her teeth, her body tensing underneath me.

I stop teasing Dani long enough to undo my zipper, sighing with relief as my cock springs free. I lower myself onto her, and she spreads her legs wider, whimpering as my erection rubs against her sex. Her panties are drenched with her arousal, and I pull them aside, sliding my cock against her juicy slit.

If I didn't want her so much, I'd tongue Dani's pussy until she soaks my face with her orgasm, but it'll have to wait. I don't even want to stop for long enough to take off her stupid thick sweater. There'll be time to get her naked and worship every supple inch, but right now, it's not gonna happen that way.

I prop myself up on one elbow and grip the base of my shaft with my other hand. I rub the head against her clit, and she shudders, her eyes closed.

"Look at me," I say. Her eyes fly open. "I'm gonna fucking pound you into this sofa because I've thought of nothing else since we met. Tell me when you're coming and look at me while you do it. You understand?"

"I understand," she gasps as I slip my cock inside her. "Do it to me."

Her ebony hair has broken free from its style, tumbling freely around her face. She looks fucking wild. She licks her lips and moans into my face as I ease into her until I rest my hips on hers, buried deep inside her clinging pussy. I reach for her thighs and pull her legs high and wide, resting my weight on them to keep her available to me. She's flexible, and her knees are almost on either side of her head.

I pull out of her and push home again, drawing a cry from Dani's throat. I dare not watch myself surging in and out of her, so I look at her face, watching as her pleasure moves her features. Her eyes are a warm hazel color, and they're fixed on mine.

She moves one hand to my lower back, pushing at me, urging me on. The other hand reaches for her pussy, and I feel my cock pulse with renewed arousal.

She's gonna touch herself.

I fucking love it when a woman takes responsibility for her own climax. It's sexy as hell to know that she wants to come just as much as I do.

Her fingertips graze my cock as she works her clit. I see her jaw clench, and her pussy does the same, clamping down on me as I slam into her. She moves her hips to meet mine, and I feel the tension building inside me.

Dani closes her eyes.

"Fucking *look* at me," I say, slowing down, "or I won't let you come."

Her eyes are wide as saucers, her mouth dropping open with indignation.

"Don't you fucking dare!" she cries, pushing her hand into my lower back as she writhes, trying to slide along my cock and keep the feeling going.

I want to deny her, and I will. *But not today.*

"Eyes on me. *Now.*"

Dani scowls as she fixes me with a stare. I move again.

"You're a fucking asshole," she says, running her fingers through my hair. She rubs her clit feverishly as I fuck her, and her back arches as her orgasm takes over.

"Oh my God," she cries. Her slick inner walls spasm and pulse as I race toward my release.

"God gets no credit here," I say, speeding up. "Whose cock is fucking you right now?"

"Yours," she says, her voice shaking.

I push her legs back even further, chasing my climax.

"Say thank you. Come on."

"Thank you, Kal," she gasps, and it's enough. I brace myself on my arms and breathe heavily as my cock twitches, emptying my come into her pussy.

I pull away, pushing my body up and away from her. There's a substantial damp patch soaking into my expensive sofa, right between those soft thighs, and I don't give a shit.

I just fucked Dani Pushkin. Probably shouldn't have. But I absolutely will do it again.

First things first.

I hold out my hand, and Dani looks at me through her heavy eyelids.

"What?" she asks.

"I'll help you to the shower. That's what you wanted, right?"

3

DANI

I'm unsteady on my feet, but Kal holds my hand as we walk to the ensuite. I sit on the edge of the bathtub as he reaches into the walk-in shower cubicle, adjusting the dial.

The water explodes from the shower head with a roar.

"Get clean," Kal says. He leaves, closing the door behind him.

My pussy throbs with aftershocks of my orgasm.

I don't know what possessed me. Never in my life have I been that obvious.

I never want a man to see how much I want him because they only take advantage and leave you feeling like an idiot when they discard you like trash. But that was undeniably a proposition on my part. I may as well have jumped on him.

I step into the flow of water. It's like standing in a monsoon. The shower head is bigger than my television screen at home, and the water pressure is good and strong. I face the wall and sigh as the stream pummels my muscles, reviving me.

I find a bottle of shower gel hanging on a hook and squeeze a generous amount into my palm. It smells of spearmint and citrus and foams up beautifully as I rub it into my skin. I slide the suds over my breasts and stomach, rinsing away the thin film of sweat that was clinging to me.

Then I feel him, his hand insistent between my shoulder blades. His lips graze my ear.

"Hands on the wall."

My pussy ought to be satiated, but it pulsates enthusiastically. What the hell is wrong with me?

The tile is smooth and cool beneath my palms. Kal places his foot between mine and bumps my ankles.

"Wider."

I see a faint cast of his reflection in the shiny surface of the wall. His hands are around my waist now, pulling me back. I shuffle back until my ass is stuck way out.

Kal's cock is hot as he rests it in the valley between my ass cheeks. He slips his length back and forth, releasing my waist so he can run his hands over my back, rinsing the soap away.

The warm water and his touch combined are priming my nerve endings, making me shake. So much sensation. It's almost too much to bear. He grasps his cock, pressing it against my pussy.

"You didn't wash here yet. You're still full of my come. I can feel it."

I feel like a complete whore, but my body is going crazy.

Five minutes ago, I couldn't imagine being horny so soon, but his touch and his filthy mouth are doing things to me.

He nudges his cock between my pussy lips and inside me, all the way to the hilt. My tits are still covered in suds, and he reaches around to grab them in his hands, my nipples hard against his palms.

He strokes in and out, long and slow.

It's not enough. I need more.

"Faster," I say. "Give it to me."

Kal lets go of my tits, and I give a yelp of shock as he grabs a handful of my hair, pulling me upright. One solid thrust propels me forward, and I catch myself on my hands before I bump my head on the wall.

I turn my head to one side, the tile cold beneath my cheek as he holds me in place, pinned to the wall. His other hand holds my hip, molding my body to his.

"You giving orders now?" he says. "You'd better be able to take what I've got for you."

Kal is a talker. His words are falling out of his mouth, assaulting my ears as he rails me.

Dirty little slut. Cock-hungry. Your pussy is mine. No one will ever make you feel as good as I do.

My tits bounce and slide with each thrust, and it's an effort to brace my legs and cope with the onslaught. But his cock is hitting all my hot spots, and I squeeze his shaft as he moves, making him groan.

"Your pussy is so tight. I'm gonna come in you again."

He puts his hands on each of my shoulders and pushes me even harder into the wall, giving him room to penetrate me even deeper.

My core heats up rapidly as my climax wracks my body. I shudder, my legs finally buckling, but Kal holds me upright by the waist. He's moving me along his cock, his thigh muscles tensing as he comes. My pussy clamps down onto him, feeling him pulsating as he empties into me.

It feels like hours later when Kal turns off the shower. He wraps me in a towel as thick as a rug, dropping a kiss on my forehead.

"Fucking beautiful," he murmurs. Then he's gone.

I rummage in the suitcase and find a t-shirt and leggings. By the time I dress and return to the bedroom, Kal is asleep. The balcony door is ajar, and the cool breeze is refreshing.

I curl up beside him, listening to the sounds of the city.

The man beside me is a total stranger.

He's still asleep, his powerful chest rising and falling rhythmically. The morning light filters through the blinds, giving the room a dreamlike haze.

I slip quietly from the bed and into the ensuite, glancing at the shower. My pussy throbs at the memory.

The dull ache in my core will be with me for days.

I open the suitcase and rummage through the outfit choices. Boot-cut jeans, a black roll-neck sweater, and some clean underwear. Everything seems to fit, which is kind of weird, although the Chelsea boots are a little on the narrow side.

I wonder how often the concierge has assembled an entire wardrobe based on nothing more than a glance at his subject. I guess Kal brings a lot of women here.

I feel a sudden wave of nausea. All that vodka on an empty stomach. Kal gave me his body but didn't give me anything to eat…

I dress quickly, scraping my hair into a high ponytail. There's a makeup palette in the suitcase, and with a quick swipe of lipstick and a fresh application of mascara, I look like an average woman rather than one who was fucked hard twice last night. I sneak into the lounge and grab my jacket.

Time to get coffee. Can you even *buy* coffee in London? Maybe it's just tea and tiny breakfast muffins. Either way, I'll bring some back for Kal.

The private elevator stops in the reception area, and the doors glide open without a sound. I glance at the lobby window and sigh.

Rain. Of course. How could it not be raining?

The girl on the desk is about my age. She smiles at me as I pass, holding out an espresso cup.

"Hey there, Miss. This is for you, it's complimentary. And don't you want any breakfast?"

I stop and frown, taking the cup from her. "What? Sorry. I don't know what you mean."

She gestures at the bar area, and I look over. On a table is a single place setting with a vase of carnations and a carafe of fresh orange juice.

"Our chef is here early. You can order anything from Huevos Rancheros to a good old English fry-up."

"Amazing," I say. "Thank you, I'm starving." I look again. "There's only one place setting, though. Isn't Kal joining me?"

"No," the receptionist says, tapping the computer, "Mr. Antonov doesn't eat in the morning."

There's a smash as the espresso shatters on the marble floor, shards of porcelain flying everywhere. The receptionist gives a yelp of surprise.

Antonov? No. Tell me I misheard her...

The receptionist is at my feet, brushing the splintered pottery into a small pan and reassuring me as she does so.

It's alright, Miss, don't worry. Accidents happen. You just take a seat, and we'll get you more coffee."

I duck down to her height and grab her shoulder. She recoils, staring at me.

"Did you say *Antonov*?"

The receptionist looks at me like she's sure I'm out of my mind. "The man whose...hospitality you've been enjoying is Mikhail Antonov, yes. He asked us to make sure you could get breakfast here this morning. Is something wrong?"

I get to my feet and stumble away towards the revolving door that leads into the street, ignoring the receptionist calling after me.

I was right the first time.

I *knew* I needed to get away from him. If I'd listened to my intuition and not my lust, I wouldn't be here now, my pussy sore from being fucked by the man who represents everything that's sick and twisted in my world.

How did he seem so normal? The devil came to me and stoked my desire, and I didn't suspect it for a moment.

I'm every bit as fucking naïve as he thinks I am.

I shove the door and almost fall over as it rotates, ejecting me onto the wet sidewalk. Knightsbridge is bustling with shoppers and commuters, jostling one another. I dash into the throng and follow the flow until I spot another hotel.

I need a phone *now*.

I peel off from the stampede and fling myself through the doors, making for the desk. A man with a name badge is standing behind it.

"Good morning—"

"Please," I say, reading his badge. "*Please*, Clive. Let me use your phone. It's an emergency."

I must be a pathetic sight. My jacket is soaked, and my hair drips onto the carpet. He beckons me with a finger and points to the door behind the desk.

"There's a phone in there. Dial zero for the operator if you're not sure of the code. Be quick."

I open the door and disappear through it before Clive changes his mind. I find the phone mounted on the wall.

When did I last use a landline? I have no idea. I dial zero and give the operator Pippa's number in New York.

It rings for a while before I hear Pip yawning down the line.

"Hellooo," she says, "who is this?"

"It's me. I need your help."

"It's three in the fucking morning! Where *are* you?"

Shit. New York is five hours behind.

"I know, babe. I'm in London. I need you to book me a flight to NYC right now."

Pip is waking up now, and she hears the urgency in my voice. "What happened? Are you alright? Why haven't you called your dad?"

I choke back a sob. *Because I've done the one thing Papa might actually disown me for.*

"I can't explain now. Just get me anything out of Heathrow. I'll go there now and check with the departures desk when I get there to find out which airline you've booked me onto."

"Okay," Pip says. "Hurry home. You're scaring me."

I hang up and go back out to the lobby. Clive is waiting for me.

"I'm sorry, but I overheard. I called you a cab."

I feel like crying. "Thank you. Why are you being so kind?"

"Because you look terrified. Whatever is going on, you need to get away, and I'm not gonna start asking questions over one bloody taxi."

"Thank you. I don't have any money, but I can..."

"Just go, love." He points at the door. "Your taxi will be outside any minute."

4

DANI

"I asked you to do a simple thing, Dani."

My father is standing by the fireplace in the lecturing posture I know so well.

"All you had to do was get back for the anniversary dinner. Why didn't you book an earlier flight?"

I avoid his eyes. "Sorry, Papa. I didn't know the weather would turn like that." I smile at him. "But the art show was amazing! I'm so inspired. It's given me the push I need to finish my exhibition pieces."

Papa's eyes soften. "I worry about you, *dorogaya*."

I love my Papa so much. His heart is in the right place, even though he isn't always great at showing it.

"I like that you still call me your sweetheart," I say.

My father won't be placated, not today. "I want to know where you were. You don't have your purse or luggage. You arrived here a full day late, and you don't seem to have an explanation that makes sense."

He's right. I don't. Because if I tell him the truth, he'll never let me out of his sight again, and all I want is to break free. To make my own way as an artist and leave this Bratva bullshit behind. I know what's in store for me if I don't.

I may be young, but I can see it all playing out before me, like a movie. I'll go the same way as my sister Mel, married to a Bratva man I barely know and locked into a life I didn't choose.

Although maybe I'm protesting too much. Unfamiliar criminals are apparently my thing if the last twenty-four hours are anything to go by...

"I told you, Papa," I say. "I was stranded in Geneva, that's all. I lost my stuff."

Papa stares at me, then sighs. "Fine. You don't want to tell me, Dani. That's up to you. "

I open my mouth to say something, but my father raises his hand sharply. This is part of our family's non-verbal shorthand, which means this conversation is over.

I leave the room and head into the kitchen, where Mama and Mel are chopping vegetables.

My mother puts down her knife. "Did it go well?" she asks.

"Nope," I reply. "He's really mad at me, and he's still deciding what he's gonna do about it."

My mother smiles and touches my cheek. "My Dani. We missed you yesterday, and now you're keeping secrets. What do you expect? You're the youngest daughter of the Pakhan, and you have to accept that this comes with expectations. If you want to play stupid games, then don't be shocked if you win stupid prizes."

I roll my eyes. "I know you're right. Please go and talk Papa down? He's working up a head of steam over it all. I'll finish this for you."

Mama leaves the kitchen, closing the door behind her. I take her place beside Mel, picking up celeriac. We say nothing for a couple of minutes, and it's understood that we're just waiting until we're sure Mama isn't coming back.

Mel speaks first.

"So," she says, slicing scallions, "what *actually* happened? Because you haven't got a good cover story this time, and you aren't your usual self. Something has rattled you, hasn't it?"

I wonder if I should lie to Mel but dismiss the idea in a heartbeat. Mel is the only person I trust even more than Pippa. They are both my best friends, but Mel is my sister too, and what's more important than family?

"I got stranded. That part is true." I stop cutting the vegetables. "But I got a ride out of there on some guy's plane. He beat up a scumbag who mugged me in the airport."

I look at Mel to see her mouth hanging open. "You're serious?" she asks. "*Shit.* Who was this mysterious hero?"

I ignore that question. "He was hot. Funny too. We had to ditch in London because of the weather, and he let me stay with him at his place."

"Oh, you *slut!*" Mel exclaims, her face splitting into a grin. "You fucked some rich sex god you just met? Tell me you got his number!"

I'm about to watch that smile fall off her face and smash to the ground, just like the espresso cup.

I draw a deep breath and take the knife from her hand. She frowns at me.

"Mel, it was Mikhail Antonov."

She claps her hand over her mouth.

"Are you fucking *insane*? Why did you do that?" Her expression darkens. "He raped you, didn't he? Tell me the truth."

"No, he didn't," I say, taking her hand. "Please listen to me. He calls himself Kal, so I never made the connection. I didn't know who he was until it was too late, and soon as I found out, I got the fuck out of there."

Mel squeezes my fingers. "Dani. Does he know who *you* are?"

I never thought about that.

"Yes. He read my name off my passport."

"He screwed you, knowing who you are. That's *sick*."

It *is* sick. I have never had sex with someone who hates me. He hid it so well, but the Antonov family is the biggest threat to my happiness. Just the name tastes foul in my mouth.

Mel is still speaking. "Mikhail's stepfather hand-chose him to claim his so-called legacy, even pushing aside his own blood. What a ruthless shit must he be if his stepfather would rather have him exact revenge than his own birth son?"

I don't want to think about *that*.

Even though I wanted Kal, even though my body was on fire for him, I now feel violated.

I slept with a man who wants to see me and mine dead. A man who, if he got the chance, would laugh with glee as my world burned down before my eyes.

Now I'm safe with my sister, the tears fall. Mel pulls me into her arms, and I rest my head on her shoulder.

"Come on, it's okay," she says, stroking my hair. "You made a mistake. But you can't tell Papa. He'd be broken if he knew an Antonov had ravaged his little girl." She pauses, stifling a giggle. "But I want to know. Was it good?"

I can't help but laugh. "Oh *God*, yes. Why is it always the bastards who are amazing in bed?"

Mel's late husband was a swine, but he had *that* going for him. Mel said his shitty personality was almost worth it for the sex. Unfortunately, other women agreed with her, and eventually, one of their husbands took offense and settled the matter at the end of a twelve-gauge shotgun.

Mel has no kids, and, as far as things go in our world, she's someone else's property, damaged goods. A Bratva widow isn't a tantalizing prospect, so she's been alone for a while now. No wonder she's interested in my escapades.

Mama appears in the doorway.

"Well, this is cozy," she says. "I won't ask what you've been up to. Dani, we need to talk to you."

Mama leads me back into the lounge, where my father is standing at the window. He's looking outside. He doesn't turn around as he speaks.

"Dani, you will not be returning to Europe, or even leaving this city, for some time."

No. *No*.

"Papa, I'm due at the Sorbonne next week. I'm booked onto a series of lectures, and I'll be doing some teaching too."

"No, you won't. You're staying here. Your exhibition is here in the city, so that's fine. You can keep that commitment. But otherwise, I'm keeping you close."

I shoot a look at my mother, and she just shrugs. I know I don't have the right to protest - after all, I'm being evasive, and it's not a good look - but I cannot *bear* to be locked down.

"Don't do this. I'll be fine. I'll check in every day."

Papa turns to face me. "You're acting like this is a debate. It isn't. Normally I give you as much freedom as I can, but if you're going to abuse that privilege, then I'm going to withdraw it. Surely that isn't so surprising?"

Of course it isn't. But it *hurts*.

"I understand," I say. "For what it's worth, I'm sorry for letting you down."

"Go home, Dani," Mama says. "Go be with Pippa for a while, and let your father calm down."

∽

I walk through the streets, fighting the wind. New York is home, and I usually love it, but it feels like a prison now.

Kal fucking Antonov. I can't believe I let that bastard touch me. I can't believe he made me feel the way he did. Even now, knowing what I know, I couldn't swear that I'd be able to resist him if he put his hands on me again.

I want out. I don't want to be a queen, married off to a Bratva king. I don't want to be tethered to this dangerous life where life is cheap and women's lives are cheaper still.

What a hypocrite I am.

So what if I liked Kal? So what if he only had to set eyes on me to nearly kill a man for daring to hurt me?

Kal is Bratva too. Our world produces only cold, brutal assholes, and he's the worst of them all. There's no love to be had within the mafia, and I'd have to lose my mind entirely to fall for a psycho like him.

So it's just as well I'll never see him again. Or at least, I hope not because if I do, he would probably be here to kill us all.

5

KAL

My mother is stirring her peppermint tea. She's been doing it for ages because she knows it drives me crazy.

Simeon and Vera sit in silence, as though they're trying to fade away and not attract her ire. I'm not so easily cowed.

My mother wants me to call her *mat'*, the formal word for 'mother,' but I refuse. 'Mama' is out of the question now that we're all adults, so we use her first name.

"Idina, I told you," I say. "I didn't know who she was."

I'm sticking with this lie for now. My mother doesn't need to know that I saw the youngest daughter of the despised Fyodor Pushkin, took a shine to her, and manipulated her straight onto my cock.

"Besides," I continue, "why the fuck do you think I'm even telling you this?"

Vera laughs.

"You are *such* a piece of shit," she says.

Idina's eyes shift from Vera to me and back again. A narrow smile stretches across her face.

"So you thought you'd get the Pushkin girl's panties in a bunch, so you can waltz in there and do the job?"

I shake my head. "No, it'll take more than that. She knows who I am, remember? She ran out on me when she found out. That's the only explanation for me waking to find her gone."

"Maybe you are just shit in bed, Kal," Simeon says.

"It's possible. But you should keep your mouth shut until you've had positive feedback on your sexual prowess from someone who doesn't ask for your credit card number beforehand."

Idina grins. She loves it when we fight. She's always worked hard to ensure that the three of us don't get close enough to gang up on her. We scrabble for scraps of her affection like starving dogs.

"Whoremongers have no opinion here, Simeon, so stop giving your brother shit over nothing. When did you last do anything useful?"

Simeon glares at her. "You mean other than being here and spying on the Pushkins instead of gallivanting around Switzerland and going balls-deep into our enemies?" He points at me. "And *he* is *not* my brother."

Vera stifles a snort of laughter and stands up, heading for the drinks cabinet. "You are *such* a loser, Simeon," she says.

"Stop whining." She looks at me over her shoulder and grins. "So spill it, half-brother. What's the plan?"

Glad you asked, little sis.

"Simeon said Danica Pushkin is using the exhibition space at The Refinery to show her art in a few weeks." I raise my eyebrows at Simeon. "Correct?"

Simeon grunts in assent.

"Fine. So that's our play."

Idina pats the chair beside her. "Come and sit here, my son," she says. Simeon is closest to her and moves towards the seat.

"Not you," she says, waving him away. "Mikhail. Come and be beside me."

I sit in the chair, and she holds out her hand. Dutifully, I take it.

"You two can go," she says. "Kal and I have important things to talk about."

Simeon mutters something as he moves toward the door. Vera shushes him, but it's too late.

"What?" Idina hisses. Simeon tries to give her an angry look, but he looks like a sad little boy.

"Nothing."

"Yes, you are," Idina says.

I close my eyes. *Jesus Christ*. Does she have to be so brutal to him?

Simeon is the scapegoat for everything that goes wrong in

our lives, and Vera exists only as a mirror image of our mother. There to be a shadow of her.

As for me, I'm Idina's golden child. The son she conceived before she met my father and raised alongside my two younger siblings.

I'm the boy who was favored and nurtured with a single goal - to help my stepfather Erik to restore his rightful place as leader of the Pushkin Bratva and push his hated, traitorous cunt of a brother out of his empire. But when I was still just a kid, Erik got impatient and made his play too soon. Fyodor Pushkin sent him back in a box.

Up until then, Erik reminded me of my destiny every single day.

To succeed where he had failed. Avenge him by killing Fyodor and taking the Bratva throne, elevating the Antonov name out of ignominy, and restoring the respect and power we deserve.

"What are you going to do, Mikhail? Idina asks.

"War does not have to involve running through the front door with your sword drawn, fighting face to face," I say. "The cunning conqueror knows that killing in hot blood may be fast, but it carries too much risk. Far better to coax and wheedle and prod at your enemy's weaknesses until they are worn down. Only then do you reveal your true intentions and deliver the murderous final blow; by then, it's almost a kindness."

Idina juts her chin at me. "I've taught you well, haven't I? Your father too. You're just as cold and black-hearted as he was. Admirable traits in a man of strength."

Idina always said she didn't know who my real father was, and she tends to disregard the fact that it wasn't Erik Antonov. She talks about me as though I'm his doppelgänger, fated to save her from the scourge of a disgraced family name.

Maybe I am. I don't know any other way to be.

I can convince anyone that I'm a regular, decent guy, at least for a short while. But I'm an agent of change. A man who defines himself by things he has yet to achieve and sees nothing beyond revenge.

I stand up and extract my hand from Idina's grasp. Her fingers are cold and bony in mine, and I'm glad to let them go.

"I'll talk to Simeon and Vera and get the wheels spinning," I say. "But I will put myself beside Fyodor Pushkin without a struggle. And when I'm sure I can get the job done, that's it. He's dead."

I head into the hallway and see that the front door to Idina's home is open. The glow of cigarettes is the only thing I can see outside on the porch.

I could do with a drink before trying to talk to my siblings. I know they'll do what I say, but they exhaust me, Simeon especially.

I don't know why my half-brother is so fucking pissed off about not being our mother's best blue-eyed boy. It's not much of a privilege. Idina has no more love for me than she does for any of us, but she likes to act as though she does to keep Simeon on his toes. Vera stopped trying years ago, and now she just keeps her head down and follows orders.

I step into the kitchen and pour myself a vodka, allowing myself a minute to think about Dani.

It was a shame to wake up and find she'd vanished. I had intended to enjoy a lazy morning with my face buried between her legs, but my morning wood went to waste.

Still, it was a fucking delicious diversion.

That woman. That tight pink pussy, those languorous moans. And such a slut for my cock. I was almost embarrassed for her. Before I could make a move, she took it there first, asking me if I wanted her.

She knew. She wanted me, too.

And to the victors go the spoils.

Maybe I can keep Dani for myself when all this murderous vengeance has run its course. I neither want nor can love her - that's for people with hearts and souls and all that shit - but I *can* fuck her. Pussy, ass, face, anything goes.

I thought she was totally innocent, but she isn't. Dani Pushkin may be only twenty years old - ten years younger than me - but her velvet-smooth, wet little cunt is craving me. I *know* it.

She will have my name and my come on her lips before long, and she'll love it.

Gotta stop thinking about her and deal with business.

"So that's clear?" I ask. Simeon and Vera both nod.

"I'll stake out the gallery and watch out for Dani," Vera says. "When she shows up, I'll call Simeon, and we'll go to work."

Simeon flicks his cigarette at Idina's favorite topiary rabbit, singeing its ear. "What if her father is there?"

"She'll arrive early to set things up," I say. "That's when you need to do it. But be fucking careful, okay? I'm not invincible and don't want to end up dead because of your incompetence."

"Heaven fucking forbid," Simeon sneers. "Can't have the anointed one scuffing his shoe or getting a hangnail, can we?"

"You wanna explain to Mommy dearest how you *accidentally*," Vera curls her fingers into exaggerated air quotes, "killed her champion? Because without Kal, we have nothing."

"What about me?" Simeon asks. "I'm Papa's son by blood. This duty should be *mine*."

Vera ruffles Simeon's hair. It's a gesture that would be affectionate in an average family, but we're something else. My sister knows it enrages Simeon, and that's the only reason she does it.

"You would have to work up to nothing, Simmi," she purrs.

Vicious bitch.

There was a time when Vera wanted better for herself, but that's over now. She wants me to be Pakhan of the Pushkin Bratva so she can get herself a high-ranking Russian man of good stock, have his babies, and do nothing of note with her life.

Then again, Bratva princesses aren't usually encouraged to aspire to anything, so it surprised me when I learned that Dani's an aspiring artist.

"Stop fighting," I scold. "You two are fucking insufferable. I'm going home now. Don't call me with your petty squabbles and *don't* wind Idina up. She's already gonna be off on her warrior queen trip tonight, and I am not sticking around for that."

I walk through the garden to the driveway and my car.

I can still hear Simeon. He's admonishing Vera for calling him Simmi. I get in the car and turn on the engine, grateful to drown them out.

Six weeks until Dani's exhibition, and then I'll have her in my sights.

No love, no feelings, no conscience.

No problem.

6

DANI

Six weeks later…

"These are *so* heavy," Pippa says, leaning a canvas against the wall. "Don't you know any attractive strongmen to come and shift them?"

"Attractive?" I ask, stacking another painting on top. "No, and my father's men have been following me for weeks. This is the first and only day that I'm getting some freedom. So the *last* thing I need is brawny goons manhandling my art."

"You're the one who needs manhandling," Pippa says with a grin. "Again."

I laugh. Pip knows the entire story of what happened with Kal, and she's convinced there's more to it. I can't get her to understand that it was a stupid mistake, and I will definitely not be seeking him out.

"Pip, Kal Antonov is a huge threat to me. Why is this so hard to grasp?"

"I think *you* want to grasp his huge, hard threat and jump on it," Pippa says. "You've been weird ever since you got back from Switzerland."

"I told you, I'm pissed off at not being able to go to Paris. And I haven't been feeling well, either."

"Whatever." Pip wraps brown paper around a canvas, securing it with string. "But I think you're fooling yourself. Would it be so bad if you and Kal got together? Might give your families something to bond over."

I sigh.

Pip is a trust-fund baby from England, and her father is a minor aristocrat. She lives in New York because she wants to, and her family pays her bills while she interns and applies to study at prestigious international schools. But although she's rich, she's not also Bratva. She does not know what a mafia feud involves, no matter how many times I explain it to her.

I decide to change the subject,

"Let's get this done before the courier arrives," I say, loading several canvases onto a handcart. "These should have been finished and in place at The Refinery two days ago."

"Are you going to be there early tonight?" Pippa asks.

"I'm gonna walk down there as soon as these last pieces are in place," I say. "It's a beautiful day, and the fresh air will do me good."

"Walk?" Pippa asks. "Who walks somewhere voluntarily?"

I smile at her. "Someone who wants to feel free, even if it's only for a short while."

~

The afternoon sunshine casts long shadows as I walk through the park. There's a bite to the air - it is October, after all - but my bouclé coat and scarf keep the chill from creeping down my neck.

It feels *so* good to be alone.

The last few weeks have been tough for all of us.

My father would not be turned, and despite my Mama and sister's efforts, he kept me under tight control. I haven't been able to do much except hang out with Pippa and work on my art, so the exhibition is now almost twice the size I expected.

My muse went on a journey, too. My canvases are usually bright, with abstract slices of yellows and whites in thick, textured oil paint. I often add gold leaf, diamond powder, and natural elements, like leaves and sand, to bring together both the earthy realness of nature and the hedonistic desires of humanity.

But lately, I'm choosing darker colors. Swathes of purple bruise the canvas, contrasting with the light but complimenting it too. I'm drawn to materials I never used before - glass, flint, thorns. Things that have to be handled with care.

Some pieces aren't going on display because they feel too personal. I finished one canvas only yesterday, a deep indigo background spliced with silvery slicks of paint. I spent hours gluing tiny pieces of broken mirror to it, arranging them in lines and swirls. The effect is disconcerting - all the viewer can see is their reflection thousands of times, and if the light hits it a certain way, it creates the occasional blinding flash.

I give little conscious thought to my art. It's an expression of my inner landscape, and too close an examination might frighten away my inspiration. It's skittish, like a baby deer.

But some work is not *just* art. It's therapy.

My thoughts tail off as I arrive at the gallery. The Refinery is closed to the public, but I know the combination to the door.

I let myself in and head upstairs. My footsteps echo as I walk through the exhibition hall.

I'm pleased that the movers have set up the space to my specification. I lay my canvases out so that they tell a story. They move from sunny to darker and more ominous as I walk by.

Is this the first sign of some impending nervous breakdown? If so, it's incredibly pretentious.

A console in the second-floor office controls the sound and lighting. I head inside, set the system to run through a playlist of eighties pop classics, and tinker with the light settings, trying out different effects. I wonder if I can work out how to change the color of the bulbs as we reach the end of the display.

∽

I've been here a while, concentrating, my tongue sticking out at the corner of my mouth. It's a simple enough interface, but bulb nine insists on being pink...

The music scrambles then cuts out. I click on the desktop player, trying to get it started again.

Then I notice a smell. I breathe in deeply, and this time I get a lungful of something acrid and toxic. I cough violently and jump up from my seat.

Burning.

Smoke is creeping under the closed door. This little room will become a gas chamber if I don't get out of here. I touch the door with my hand to see if it's hot.

No. That means the fire isn't directly outside.

I open the door slowly, only to be hit in the face with smoke. My eyes stream and I'm hacking away, my throat closing as I move towards the stairs.

Get down on the ground. Get under the smoke.

I lie on my stomach and commando-crawl to the top of the stairwell. I can't see anything for a moment, but then my eyes adjust a little, and the full extent of the danger I'm in is clear.

The first floor is an inferno. I have no idea how it could have gotten to this stage so fast without me noticing, but there's no way I can get out. The heat is so intense that I can feel it drying out my eyes and throat, and I close my mouth, trying not to throw up as I swallow the particles of burning paint and plastic in the air.

I'm gonna die I'm gonna die I'm gonna die I'm gonna—

Fire exit. There is one on this floor. A door to a metal staircase outside. Where?

My thoughts are falling over each other as though they all want to get their turn before I lose consciousness.

The sprinklers didn't come on. Is anyone coming to put the fire out? All my work is gone. I didn't tell my Mama and Papa that I love them today.

I never even fell in love.

I'm halfway along the landing, the glow of the fire exit sign just visible before me. But I won't make it. My limbs are leaden, and my body settles to the floor as though I'm just in need of a good nap, and *then* I might try to escape.

My mind throws one more thought at me as it shuts down.

I never saw Kal again.

I close my eyes.

It'll be over soon.

7
DANI

My body convulses, and I sit up involuntarily, heaving as I do so. My stomach feels like it might hurl itself out of my mouth. I punch my chest, trying to cough up what feels like a boulder lodged in there.

Strong arms grip me, and I realize I'm being carried. My eyes are so sore that I can't see anything when I open them.

"I'm blind," I croak. "Help me."

"I *am* helping you," a voice replies. "Just hold on, Dani."

I blink hard, trying to clear my vision.

I recognize that voice.

This is a joke. I'm already dead.

"Kal?" I wheeze. "How did you? I mean, why are you... what's..."

"Shh," Kal says. "Stop trying to talk. You're hurt."

I have no energy to protest. I drop my head against his shoulder and feel the softness of his shirt against my face.

It has to be a dream. *What the fuck* is he doing here?

I can see the hazy shapes of the firefighters as they tackle the blaze. The oldest gallery in the district has gone forever, taking all my work with it.

It shouldn't matter. At least I'm alive. But the exhibition was my chance to be recognized as an artist. Doors would have opened for me. I could have moved on, broken free, and been known as more than criminal royalty.

I'll be associated forever with this disaster, and the art community is superstitious. It was hard enough to be judged on my merits without giving people another excuse to turn away from me.

I squeeze my eyes closed again, a fresh wave of pain in my head. Kal lays me down, his jacket underneath me. My body feels stiff, and I shiver.

A firefighter appears at my side.

"Shit," he says, touching my face. "That was close." He turns to Kal. "You need an ambulance here, buddy. She looks like she'll be okay, but you gotta get her looked over."

Kal's voice is edged with steel. "You could have said all that without putting your hands on her. Now back the fuck off."

"Okay, you got it." The firefighter raises his hands and moves away.

Kal turns back to me. "So, Dani. Do I have to be there every time you get in trouble?"

I don't have time to respond. A man's voice is yelling.

"Mikhail Antonov," he shouts. "Get the fuck away from my daughter."

Kal stands up quickly. From the look on his face, I guess he's realized who is approaching us.

I knew from the moment I heard his voice.

Papa.

~

My father is right there, my mother and sister in tow. He was probably expecting to find me dead or on my way to the hospital.

Papa squares up to Kal and shoves him in the chest. Brutus, my father's bodyguard, pulls out his gun and jams it against Kal's temple.

"Woah," Kal says, taking a large step back. "Calm down, old man."

Papa takes in Kal's singed jacket and soot-covered face. He turns away and bends down to me as I sit up on my knees.

"*Dorogaya*, what happened? Tell me."

I cough hard, spitting out a mouthful of black gunge.

I'm starting to come around now, and I know I need to mind my words. Because until I work out what the hell is going on, it won't do any good for my father to find out that this isn't the first time Kal Antonov has saved me.

"He came in and carried me out of the fire. I passed out on the upstairs landing." I frown. "Wait. How did you get here so quickly, anyway?"

It takes Papa too long to answer, and he looks away, catching Mama's eye.

"Oh, I *see*. Someone was spying on me. After you said you'd leave me be today, you sent your people to watch me?"

"Well, was I so wrong?" Papa snaps. "Look at this!" He waves his hand at the burning building. "You could have been a charred corpse!"

My father stands up and faces Kal. "And as for *you*—"

"As for me *what*, Fyodor?" Kal says. He doesn't react at all to Brutus's gun, but instead, he's focused on my father. "I ran in there and saved your daughter. Whatever you think of me, that's a fact."

"You bastard Antonovs aren't welcome within a million miles of my family or me," Papa says, jabbing his finger in Kal's face. "You *know* that. So why are you here?"

I'm interested in the answer to this question too.

Kal sighs and places a hand on his chest as though he's swearing to something.

"I left my family, Fyodor. I want nothing to do with them anymore."

My father narrows his eyes but says nothing. The light of the fire bathes them both in a demonic reddish glow, and for a moment Kal looks like Lucifer, beseeching God for mercy.

Kal shows Papa his hands. "I come to you with nothing. No one else is here. I hoped to see you at the exhibition and was here early, that's all."

My father nods at Brutus, and he lowers his gun to his side but doesn't holster it.

"Fine," Papa says. "Go." He turns away, reaching for my hand.

"You don't understand, Fyodor," Kal says. "I know you always thought it'd be me who would start a fight. But my family will remain dangerous. Idina will never stop trying to get to you. Losing me won't deter her for long."

Kal moves quickly and grabs my outstretched hand before Papa does. He pulls me to my feet, and I yank my hand away, glad to retreat to my mother's arms.

"I want to work for you," Kal says. "I want to earn my place in this family. We were all Pushkins once."

"*You* weren't," Mel says. "You weren't born of this family. You're not a Pushkin by blood."

Just as well, after what we did in London...

"Exactly correct, Melania," Kal continues. "None of you actually know me. We have no personal quarrels. So why should I be punished for the sins of the Antonovs when *I* committed no crime against you?"

Mama and Mel both look at Papa. He's glaring at Kal, his nostrils flaring with rage at his impudence.

"Get away from us," Papa says. "We want nothing to do with you, and you can be a lone wolf or die in the gutter for all I care."

My mother is speaking.

"Fyodor," she says, releasing me from her embrace and taking a step towards my father, "he saved Dani's life. He came to us with empty hands, no tricky deals, nothing. We have a code of honor, do we not?"

My father closes his eyes and exhales long and slow. "Marta. This is *Mikhail Antonov*. What the fuck are you talking about?"

"You owe him a blood debt. Your youngest child survived because this man risked his own life saving hers." Mama touches my father's arm. "Fyodor. Let's all go home and look after Dani. We should take Kal with us, and you need to hold your judgment." Mama nods at Kal. "The boy makes a good point about the danger his family represents. When they realize he's with us, they may be minded to retaliate, and we need him to keep them at bay."

Mama knows that my father is a stickler for doing the 'right' thing and upholding the standards and traditions that mean so much to him.

Papa gives her a hard look, but she's got the upper hand.

"Brutus, it's all right, *tovarishch*," he says.

Brutus holsters his gun, and there's an uneasy silence. Kal offers my father a handshake.

Papa looks at Kal's hand for a long moment before turning away and striding towards the cars, Brutus falling into step beside him. Kal shrugs and looks at me, and despite the situation, a broad grin lights up his face as he speaks.

"I think he likes me."

8

KAL

All I want to do is look at Dani, but I don't want to get caught staring. The situation is febrile enough with us all in the limo together. But the occasional glance is better than nothing, and I try to drink her in.

Her face is smudged with greasy black marks from the smoke, and she has a graze on her cheek. The black shift dress is still intact, but her pantyhose are shredded, runs laddering up her legs. She lost both shoes along the way, too.

Her hair is a rat's nest, and I'm reminded of the last time I saw it looking like that. When she was coming on my cock.

We arrive, and everyone ignores me as we go into the house. I stand awkwardly in the hallway as Marta Pushkin leads Dani upstairs.

"Bed for you," she says. "The doctor will come and see you as soon as we can get him here."

I watch Dani's pert ass as she climbs the stairs, her legs faltering beneath her. She's arguing in a weak, strained voice.

"You need to call Pippa, Mama..."

"I will," Marta says. "I'll get Mel to deal with all that."

The door to the bedroom closes, and I can hear nothing except the ticking of the grandfather clock. I remove my jacket and hang it on the coat stand.

I'm admiring a bust of Marcus Aurelius when Fyodor appears in a doorway.

"Come here," he barks.

I obey and find myself in a library. There are several Chesterfield armchairs, a table for playing cards, tall bookshelves, and the ubiquitous drinks cabinet.

I smile. Every Bratva house has alcohol available in most rooms. I could probably open the bathroom cupboard and find a row of miniature bottles, just right to throw back while I'm having a piss.

"Nice," I say, looking around the room. "Who's the reader?"

Fyodor is in no mood for small talk.

"Shut up," he says. "I wanna know one thing. Are my family in real danger? Is Idina planning to unleash hell on us?"

You stupid old fuck. Yes, she is. You're looking at it. And you invited it into your fucking home like an idiot.

"Yes, she's a threat," I say. "You need me here, believe me."

A thought occurs to me, and I almost punch the air in jubilation.

"She's probably gonna try to hurt Dani," I continue, picking up an ashtray and turning it over in my hand. The words 'Greetings from Minsk' are etched into it.

"So when did you last visit the Motherland?" I ask. I suppress a smirk as Fyodor glares at me.

"Stick to the fucking point," he snarls. "Idina wants to hurt my Dani?"

No, not particularly. But you're so overprotective, you're gonna eat up this bullshit like it's steak au poivre, *and the rest will be easy.*

And I will get to have my fun.

"Idina thinks Dani is an easy target. She was alone today, and look what almost happened. A Bratva princess needs a security detail at all times."

I look at Fyodor's face as he digests my words. It's so satisfying, watching him as my idea rolls around in his head before settling into his consciousness. It's like when you pot a pool ball with a trick shot.

"All right, Kal," Fyodor says. "You can take that role. You know your mother best, making you Dani's best line of defense."

"You got it."

Fyodor extends a hand to me. "I'll take that handshake, boy. For now, I'm listening to my wife and reserving judgment."

I shake his hand, and he lets go quickly, heading for the door.

"Marta will make up a room for you. There's food in the kitchen."

∽

The dead of night, and the house is silent.

I still can't believe how easy it was to get into the belly of the beast. The Pushkins are not what I expected - they seem incredibly trusting. Too ready to take what I say at face value.

If she had been in Fyodor's shoes, my mother would have shot me in the face and laughed about it. Well, more fool him. I'm Dani's bodyguard and have a legitimate reason to be at her side. Her opinion on the matter is meaningless.

I try not to think about the fact that the t-shirt and sweatpants I'm wearing most likely belong to Fyodor. Gotta get some new clothes and fast. Luckily, the house is warm, and I strip out of the t-shirt, dumping it on the rug beside the bed.

The room is not entirely dark. Everything looks indigo except when the moonlight filters through the thin drapes, throwing silvery highlights onto the furniture.

I heard the doctor come and go. He wasn't here long, so I assume Dani is doing okay.

My cock swells at the thought of her in her bed, warm, safe, and waiting for me. She's only alive because I rescued her.

I wonder if she's grateful.

Thank you, Kal, she gasped as she came. God, I wanna make her come again. I want to reduce her to a quivering, needful mess, good for nothing until she gets her fill of my cock.

Like most bad people, I can sniff out weaknesses in others and use them to get what I want. And when she leaned back on my sofa and asked me if I wanted to fuck her, I learned something important.

Dani's weakness is *me*. She just doesn't know it yet.

I get out of bed and make my way across the bedroom, feeling my way carefully and listening out for squeaky floorboards. I make no sound, and I'm outside Dani's door within a minute.

A lock. And not just any lock - it's a panic room setup, a keypad interface with numbers. I've seen this style before, and Dani can open it from the inside unless someone outside locks her in.

A red light blinks in the darkness, letting me know I'm going no further.

The numbers glow, mocking me. There are ten thousand combinations to be made with digits zero through nine, and that's if she only used the minimum of four to make up her code.

I close my eyes and think.

Dani isn't protecting a bank vault. It's just her bedroom. And the override hasn't been activated, so her parents can get in, meaning it must be a code *they* can remember too.

I try to visualize the numbers beside Dani's face. The passport photo, and right there, her date of birth. I remember it because the date is less than a week from now.

It's the stupidest, most obvious choice for a passcode. These idiot Pushkins never considered the possibility that someone other than Dani's family might try to get in her room and might know her fucking birthday.

The digits come to me in a flash, and I don't waste time second-guessing myself. I'm decisive, and I trust my instincts. I tap the keypad, and the red light turns green.

Bingo.

I ease the door open and wince, waiting for a creak, but there's nothing. I enter the room and close the door behind me.

The room is lit by a Himalayan salt lamp, which emits a warm orange glow on the bedside table. In bed, Dani is sleeping.

I move to the foot of the bed and watch her for a while.

The graze on her cheek is covered with a gauze square, held in place with surgical tape. Her hair is clean and braided to keep it off her face.

The sight of her injured face makes me seethe. I don't know where that's coming from, but I want to find Simeon and break his jaw for what he did, even though it was my idea.

My half-brother must have used a shit-ton of gasoline to make the place go up like that. Even accounting for all that open space and the sprinkler system being sabotaged, it caught like kindling. I had to run like hell back down the fire exit to escape the traveling flames, and it was fucking hard work to do that while carrying an unconscious woman.

I can never truly be sure that Simeon won't kill me if he gets the chance. Vera too. The only thing that stops them is fear of Idina's reaction. But when I'm running the Pushkin Bratva, all of them will bow to me, my mother included.

Dani stirs and slides one long leg out from beneath the sheets. My mouth goes dry at the sight of her flawless ivory skin, pale despite the orange light.

My cock is throbbing in my sweatpants, and I grasp it through the fabric. I want to jerk off right here, marking her with my come and claiming her as mine.

I sit on the edge of the bed and trail my finger along Dani's thigh. She whimpers, but her eyes remain closed. She rolls onto her back and parts her legs a little, and as the bed linen shifts, I see that she's only wearing panties and a camisole.

My common sense sounds klaxons, rings bells, anything to get my attention, but it's all in vain.

Don't do it. If she wakes up, she'll scream the house down, and you'll get murdered.

I lean down and reach into the dark valley between Dani's thighs, finding the softness of her panties. Her pussy is warm beneath the fabric, and as I press my thumb between her pussy lips, she moves her hips and moans.

My thumb feels damp as I push harder, finding her clit. Her juice soaks through the cotton, and I want to pull her panties aside and taste her.

Dani is still asleep or pretending to be, but her body betrays her. I gather the fabric in my hand and pull it into her slit, using it to tease her clit. My other hand is working my cock.

I have to stop. I have to. I won't get away with this...

Dani's eyes are open.

I freeze. As I watch, her eyes slowly close again, and her body relaxes.

That was way too fucking close.

I let go of her panties and tuck my raging erection into my waistband before stealing out of the room. I re-arm the door lock and return to my bed.

I lie on my back. The ceiling of my room looks the same as it did ten minutes ago, but it feels like the rest of the world has shifted.

She's just a woman. A beautiful, feisty woman with foxy eyes and a body that drives me crazy. But still just a woman.

There will be time for games, but I need to keep hold of the reins. One clear chance to kill Fyodor Pushkin, and then all his treasures are mine, his pretty daughter included.

I close my eyes and wait for sleep.

9

KAL

I get up early because I know Fyodor does the same.

Simeon is an excellent little sneak, and he's watched the Pushkins for years. So I know Fyodor likes breakfast and newspapers in the lounge before he sees to business.

When I arrive downstairs, the only person around is Marta. She's in the kitchen, filling a giant coffee pot.

"A lot of visitors this morning," she says, "and all of them need caffeine. People ask Fyodor for favors every day, and it takes a while for him to get around to everybody."

Damn. So the Pushkin patriarch is safe for now.

"What takes so long?" I ask, pouring myself a cup. "'No' is a complete sentence. What more is there to say?"

Marta cocks her head at me and frowns. "Kal, two things. First, Fyodor prefers to say *yes* as much as possible because treating people well is how a Pakhan maintains the trust and respect of people around him. And second, who are you to criticize? Your stepfather allowed ambition to swallow his soul and squandered everything good in his life. Look where it got him. Cold in the ground."

I sip my coffee while I think of a neutral response, but inside, I'm furious.

Erik was a *strong* man. He had the ruthless edge that a leader needs. None of this talking-it-out bullshit with subordinates. Erik took what he wanted and gave nothing, which is why *he* should be on the Bratva throne.

"I hoped to talk to Fyodor," I say. "We got off on the wrong foot. I'd like to have his counsel, one-to-one."

"He's in meetings all morning." Marta gives me a small smile. "Is it urgent?"

Not urgent, no. But a few minutes alone with him will be enough time for me to strangle the old bastard and take off before anyone realizes what happened.

They'll figure it out quickly, but they will have a *serious* problem by then.

There will be only one legitimate claim to the Pushkin Bratva.

Me.

When a pretender murders a king, his subjects do not rise and crush the upstart. They know the kingdom's interests would crumble like sandcastles without a leader to hold them together.

Marta Pushkin believes in loyalty. She thinks her precious husband has friends. But a Pakhan only has associates, people who benefit from maintaining a relationship with him. All human interaction works the same way. We pretend we love each other, but it's all just a means to an end.

Unlike most, I choose not to live in denial.

With no one in charge, everyone would fall to squabbling. All the shitty little hustles they have going on would fade away to nothing, and they'd be left without support or investment to prop them up. So Fyodor's 'friends' will sit before me in this mansion, in the same lounge, and ask for my patronage.

"There'll be time for you to have an audience with my husband," Marta says, "but later. As for Dani, she won't be up until after lunchtime as the doctor advised her to take some bed rest."

There's no way that dirty girl was asleep while I did those things to her. She just didn't want to say anything, and neither did I.

It felt like a spell or hypnosis or something. A single word could have been enough to blow the moment away forever, leaving us with nothing but grim reality.

Marta is staring at me.

"Oh. You mean I don't need to hang around guarding her?"

"Exactly," she says. "So don't lurk in here, cramping my style. Go do something productive with your time." She holds out a key. "Here. You can take a car from the garage, and when Fyodor loses his shit about it, I'll take the blame."

∼

I wander outside. The sunshine is warming the garden, releasing the scent of jasmine into the air.

My sister Vera liked jasmine flowers.

We used to have a floral border similar to this one, and when she was a little kid, my sister tended it lovingly. On her church confirmation day, she was ready early and decided to give her flowers a drink while she waited for Idina.

Vera went into the garden with her little watering can and poured water over the jasmine patch that got the most sun. I still remember her singing as she went about her work, not noticing that her white patent shoes were getting covered in soil.

She never saw our mother approaching until it was too late.

Idina grabbed Vera's arm and dragged her onto the path, cursing at her about the state of her shoes. The poor kid was bewildered, but she knew better than to cry. Like Simeon and me, she wasted oceans of tears on our mother before learning it was pointless.

Vera could do nothing but watch as Idina crouched down and pulled handfuls of jasmine flowers up by the stems, dragging the delicate roots from the earth.

"You made me do this!" she shrieked at Vera. "After everything I do for you. I buy you a beautiful church outfit, and you hurt me like this by ruining it?"

Vera stammered when she was upset.

"M-m-m-m..."

"Mur mur mur!" Vera yelled. "Be quiet. Brush off your shoes and get in the car."

We sat quietly in church, watching as the priest gave Vera into God's care. She was as still as a mannequin, her face mask-like as she went through the motions.

We all knew God wouldn't protect us.

Vera hasn't stammered since, and she never cries either.

My cell phone buzzes in my pocket, shattering the bitter memory. I look at the caller ID.

Speak of the devil.

I walk away quickly in case someone overhears, and it's not until I round the hedge at the end of the path that I slide the button to green.

"Idina," I say. "Good morning."

"Simeon and Vera watched the whole thing. You got Dani out and left with Fyodor, so what's happening? Is he dead yet?"

Oh, hi there, Kal. How are you? Not injured or anything after running into a burning building?

"No, he is not dead yet, for fuck's sake. I will kill him when I can do it and escape. I need to come back and take control when emotions aren't running as high."

And, coincidentally, it may be a while before I get my chance to murder Fyodor, so I'll just have to spend my time fucking Dani through the wall...

"Don't mess around," Idina snaps. Then her voice changes to an unctuous, simpering tone, as though her words are dripping with syrup. "You are doing so well, my son. You make me very proud, you know that?"

I know she's manipulating me, but the child inside puffs his chest out with pride.

My Mama is proud of me.

"I will get this done, I promise," I say.

The sharp tone is back, like a kick in the balls. "Make sure you do."

There's a click, and she's gone.

I go to the garage and point the key at the many cars parked there, pressing the button. There's a clunking sound, and all the lights flash on the Alfa Romeo.

I get into the car and head for the city.

10

DANI

I feel him before I see him.

I dreamed about him last night. It was so *vivid*. His hand on my pussy, touching me, saying nothing. When I woke up, I would have believed it was real except for the fact that my door was still locked. But my panties were wet, and I had to take a minute to give myself some relief before getting out of bed.

There's something elemental about Kal Antonov. He is sure-footed in a manner that seems perverse, considering he's in my family home. Walking across the grass towards me, it feels like he's always been here.

I pull the throw tightly around my shoulders as he reaches me. Despite everything, I'd be lying if I said I wasn't pleased to see him.

Kal sits beside me on the bench. Neither of us says anything for a moment.

"So this is awkward as fuck," Kal says, running his hand through his hair. I'm struck by a sudden desire to touch him.

"It is. Why were you at the gallery?"

"Like I told your father - I was coming to see the exhibition. But if I were inclined to think about it, I'd admit I wanted to see you before your family and the other guests arrived."

I fold my page and close the book, setting it on my knee. Kal picks it up.

"*Dracula*. Appropriate for the season."

"It's my favorite book," I say. "Have you read it?"

"No. I don't read."

I scowl. *What kind of Neanderthal doesn't fucking read?*

"Look," I say, crossing my legs away from him, "I owe you my gratitude for saving my life, but it doesn't make up for what you did."

If Kal notices my body language, he doesn't care. He leans closer, those cold blue eyes piercing me.

"What do I need to make up to you?" he asks. "Because if I remember correctly, I fucked you until you were screaming, and then you squirted all over my sofa. I should invoice you for that."

My mouth is hanging open. *Get a hold of yourself, Dani.*

"Invoice me for what, the sex? That would explain a lot. "

He wrinkles his nose. "Cute. But I meant the dry cleaning for my upholstery. And the clothes I got you, the chef to make your breakfast...."

"I didn't eat it. Because I found out your last name, and funnily enough I lost my appetite."

Kal shrugs. "You didn't ask. It was a harmless lie of omission. And besides, I'm here now, ready to make your life miserable."

I eyeball him warily. "Why? What are you going to do?"

"Jesus, Dani. Where is the fucking *trust*?"

He removes his jacket, and I try to ignore the open neck of his shirt. Given that I've seen him naked, you'd think it'd be easy not to ogle him, but I can't help it.

"Your father has assigned me to guard you. How fun is that?"

"I don't need a guard," I say. "It's *you* I need to be protected from, anyway."

"I think it's me who's in danger," Kal says, smiling. "You wanted my cock inside you from the start. You told me that. I wouldn't be surprised to find out you missed the flight deliberately so that you could try to get with me."

His arrogance makes me want to fucking punch him, but I'm also aware of the warmth in my core. He wants me to think about the night we had together, and here I am trying to brush it off like I haven't relived it a thousand times.

If he only knew how often I wandered away into lewd fantasies when I was supposed to be painting. The times I retired to my bedroom with my trusty dildo, trying to feel it as well as remember it. But a silicon stick cannot live up to a real man, and most men aren't as real as Kal.

I wonder if I'm in a coma. In the hospital, half-dead from smoke or burns, and Kal is a weird sexual fever dream.

If this was some crappy romance novel, maybe. But my lungs are still scratchy. And although I took off the gauze, my face aches where a bruise is blossoming beneath the abrasion.

So yeah, I'm awake. And Kal Antonov is here. If my father wants him to follow me around, there's nothing much I can do other than accept it.

With my art destroyed, I'm back at the beginning, only worse because Papa is paranoid and fearful for the family's safety. It's as though I was playing Chutes & Ladders, and I landed on a chute just before the winning square. But instead of returning me to the start of the game, it dumped me off the fucking board entirely.

Okay. I will cope somehow. Get back to work. Create. I'll get out of this life, even if I have to claw and scrape every inch of the way.

I will get away.

"No, you won't."

Did I say that last bit *aloud*?

I turn to face Kal. I move closer to him, and he grins, seeing my anger.

"Fuck you," I say, my index finger an inch from his nose. "You know nothing about me or my life."

"I know you're a Bwatva pwincess," he says, "so don't you wowwy your pretty head about a *thing*."

The mocking baby voice is going too far. Without thinking, I pull back my hand, ready to slap him.

Kal's reflexes are lightning-quick. As my hand moves towards his face, he snatches at the air and catches my wrist. He holds it to the bench, deftly covering our hands with the fur.

"Ow!" I cry. "You fucking *zhivotnoye*. Let go!"

Kal breathes deeply, inhaling my scent. His lips are beside my ear.

"You calling me an animal? You're damn right." He grips my wrist tighter. "I will *never* let go, Dani. You're mine."

My heart hammers in my chest. *What the fuck?*

"You and I have *nothing* between us," I hiss. "You're poison."

Kal's lips graze my neck, his breath warm on my skin. "Until you knew my name, you wanted everything I had to give. And I would have let you have it, in every slutty hole, until you were drunk on my come and still begging for more."

I feel faint.

No one ever spoke to me this way before. I've had a few short flings, but men my age are all quantity and not quality. Too excitable. Who wants sex with someone who brings that Labrador puppy energy to the bedroom?

"My name means nothing," he continues, stroking my wrist with his thumb, "and neither does yours. I'm a man, and you're a woman. That's all there is to it." He bites my earlobe, and I shudder. "And believe me when I say this, Dani - I *will* have you again. I'm going to fucking ruin you.

And even if you hate me, I know you want me. Ain't that a bitch?"

Kal is whispering these wicked things to me, and my pussy is acting out *badly*. It's twitching like crazy, and all he's doing is talking...

Brutus is shouting my name.

Kal releases my wrist and moves away just as Brutus comes into view.

"Dani, your father asked me to remind you about your lesson."

Kal bursts into laughter. "Is this some Jane Austen shit?" he says to me. "Do you have a governess? Is she worth a fuck?"

A flare of jealousy lights up my anger before I consciously process what Kal said.

Dani, you can't get pissy because he might want to screw a fictional governess that you haven't got...

"Wait," I say. "You said you don't read."

"My mother likes to watch costume dramas, which means I sometimes have to watch them too."

"Well, for your information, *I* am learning how to shoot." I sit up a little taller. "My Papa wants me to get good at it. And it's fun."

Kal grins. "Your Papa sees what I see - that you're too sheltered to survive in this world of ours."

Oh, don't you fucking dare...

"Not that it's any of your business, but I don't intend to stay in this world."

Kal nods. "Fair enough. I hear Saturn is beautiful at this time of year."

Brutus chokes back a laugh and turns it into a cough.

"You aren't fooling anyone," I say to him. "You don't need to drive me. Apparently, Kal has to accompany me everywhere, so we'd better get it over with." I turn to Kal. "Any possibility of you just driving the car and not being a prick for a while?"

"Possibility?" he replies, getting to his feet. "Sure. But I promise you nothing."

11

DANI

Sergei frowns as we walk through the door. He's been coaching me in pistol accuracy off and on for about a year, and he's only ever seen me with Brutus.

Kal looks around the range.

"So we're the only ones here?" he asks.

Sergei nods. "*Da*. You, me, and Dani, until the late class starts at five p.m." He folds his arms. "Who are you, anyway? You look familiar."

"Kal Antonov."

Kal looks like he's considering offering Sergei a handshake, but he decides against it. The two men eyeball each other.

"Hello?" I say, waving my hand between them. "I'd love it if you two could stop flirting for long enough to set me up?"

Sergei heads for the armory, catching Kal's shoulder as he passes him. He wanted it to look accidental, but we all know it wasn't. Kal raises an eyebrow at me, and I shrug.

"You make friends everywhere you go, don't you? *Such* a ray of sunshine."

Kal scowls. "That fucker didn't look pleased to see me. He's got a thing for you."

"Nah," I say, rolling my eyes, "I think it's *you* he has a thing for. Look how flustered he got. And come to think of it, you seem a bit riled, too." I tilt my head at the door. "I can just go?"

Kal isn't amused. "Very fucking funny. But I'll be keeping a close eye on him because I don't like him."

"Methinks the lady doth protest too much?" I say, nudging him.

"Jesus." Kal massages his forehead with his fingertips. "You're giving me a headache."

Sergei reappears, my practice pistol in hand. He leads me out of the kit area and into the range, where he set up the targets ready for me.

Kal leans against the back wall and looks at his phone.

"Hey," Sergei says to him. "You need ear defenders."

Kal glares at him. "Do I?"

"I'm supposed to insist, but if you want to be a cunt about it, you just carry on."

Kal reaches for his ear and extracts a black earpiece, holding it out to Sergei.

"Filtering, not canceling," he says. "So I can hear speech as long as it's close, but the gunshots are muffled." He puts the earpiece back in. "*Spetsnaz* standard issue. Where are *yours*?"

"You were in the Special Forces?"

"Do you think I'd tell you if I was?"

Sergei decides he's had enough and turns back to me.

"Now, Dani," he says. "Your stance needs work. Remember what I told you? Your feet should be shoulder-width apart, with the foot opposite your dominant hand about a step past the other foot." He places his hand on my shoulder as I move into the correct position. "Great. Now lean forward with your knees bent, ensuring you're firmly balanced."

I glance over my shoulder to see Kal staring intently. But it's not me he's looking at.

I get it.

Sergei has his hands on me, and Kal isn't happy about it.

What a shame.

I look straight at Sergei and give him my best silly-girl simper.

"Are my feet right now?" I ask.

I know they're not because I shifted my front foot too far back. Oopsie.

"*Nyet, milaya,*" Sergei says. "Here." He puts his hands on my hips, turning me slightly so he can help me move.

"Let go of her."

Sergei and I turn our heads in unison to see that Kal is behind us, removing his earbuds.

"Back off, *tovarishch*," Sergei says.

Kal puts his hands in his pants pockets. His voice is low and even, but it still gives me a chill.

"It's important to me you take your hands off her right now. *Do* it."

Sergei releases my hips and faces Kal. The two men are almost nose to nose.

"Look," he begins, "I don't know what your problem is—"

Kal's head jerks forward, smashing his forehead into Sergei's nose.

Sergei falls to the ground, clutching his face as blood soaks his t-shirt.

"You can't teach Dani to defend herself," Kal shouts over Sergei's cries. "I was a threat to you from the moment I walked through the door, and you didn't even notice."

Kal takes off his jacket and hangs it on a hook on the wall.

"I will do your job for you," he says, "and you can fuck off and get cleaned up. You look like a squeezed donut."

Sergei gets to his feet and walks away without looking back, slamming the door behind him.

I'm frozen to the spot, still holding the pistol. Kal looks me up and down.

"To be fair to the guy, he was right. Your stance *is* shit."

He unbuttons his left cuff and rolls up his sleeve, frowning at the targets as he does so.

"This is *not* what you need to learn, Dani," he says. "But don't worry. I'll teach you."

He fucked up Sergei just for touching me.

Was it necessary? No. But *God*, it was hot.

Because he's not just protecting me. He knew I wasn't in danger.

I will never let go, Dani. You're mine.

That's what he said.

I don't want to *belong* to anyone. I want to be *mine*. But if Kal wants to possess me, do I have any say?

I try to ignore the voice inside because she's a thirsty bitch.

Look at him rolling up his sleeves. You're going slowly crazy for him. If you have no choice, Dani, why not just enjoy it?

I shake my head, trying to knock the thoughts out.

"What do I need to learn? I ask.

Kal smiles. "That's a hell of a question, and maybe I'll answer it more comprehensively another day. But for self-defense, you need to learn Systema."

"And that is…?"

"Kinda like Krav Maga, but different."

"Oh, so it's martial arts?"

Kal nods. He takes the gun from my hand and empties the clip before handing it back to me. "Just in case. Now, point the gun at me."

We're a few feet apart. I level the pistol at him, and he raises his hands in surrender. "Good girl," he says, and I draw a sharp breath.

I wish I didn't like it so much when he says that.

He beckons me with one hand. "Now, advance on me."

I move towards him. I'm holding the gun with both hands, one on the handle and trigger and one to hold steady.

Kal lunges at me so fast that he's a blur. Before I can register what's happening, he throws his arm in front of my face and flings it to one side, forcing my steadying hand to let go. The hand holding the gun flails away, and Kal grabs my wrist, holding it aloft. His other hand travels across my field of vision and plucks the pistol from my hand, sending it skittering along the floor and out of reach.

"And *that*," he says with a laugh, "is what you need to do with guns, Dani. You get rid of them. You'll never learn how to dodge bullets."

I'm breathing heavily, right in his face. He's not letting go of my wrist, and we're frozen in place as though we stopped mid-tango.

"You're scary, Kal. You know that?"

Kal surprises me by wrapping his arm around my waist and pulling me close. He leans in and brushes his mouth on mine, running his tongue along my lower lip.

"Fucking right I am. You wanna get out of here?"

12

KAL

We're steaming up the windows pretty fucking quickly. Even if there were anyone here, they wouldn't be able to see into the car.

But I couldn't care less either way, and Dani doesn't seem to give a shit either.

We're in the back seat. Luckily, the car is a spacious sedan, and the seats lie flat at the touch of a button.

Dani leans back on her hands and points her feet toward me.

"Shoes off," she says.

I pull at her boots, throwing them into the footwell. She's undoing the zipper of her jeans, peeling them down her legs.

Her urgency does it for me. It's as though she dares not stop and think because if she does, she might remember that the man she's so hot for is the absolute worst.

Her jeans and panties are off. I place my face in between her legs and inhale deeply.

Her scent is heady and primal. It makes me want to bury my face in her pussy and drink her up.

I nuzzle her inner thigh, and her hand reaches down, grabbing my hair.

"Come up here and kiss me first," she says.

I rarely enjoy kissing. Too personal. It falls into lovemaking territory and makes women go weird in the head, which I can do without.

But Dani doesn't have to ask me twice.

I pull myself up and along her body, lying on top of her. She tilts her head back to meet my lips. She moves her mouth against mine gently, but there's a playfulness to her kisses, and now and then, she bites my lip before running her tongue along it.

"You," I murmur against her cheek, "are looking for trouble."

"I can't help it," she whispers. "Look where we are. Anyone could catch us. What if Sergei tells my father what happened?" She catches my lip again with her teeth. "But I'm *so* turned on, Kal."

So this girl enjoys taking risks, does she? Fyodor's precious angel is something of an exhibitionist. Who knew?

I shift against Dani's pussy, grinding my erection against her as I kiss her neck.

"I'm tempted to bury my cock in you right now," I say. "But I won't." I sit on my heels to slide my pants down to my knees.

My cock is almost painfully hard, the head purplish and slick. I grasp it at the base, squeezing.

Dani is staring. She scrambles into a seated position before me, removing her shirt and bra as she does so. Her alabaster skin looks incredible against the black leather seat.

I take her chin in my hand and tip her head back.

"Open your mouth, *milaya*. I wanna see you take all of me."

Dani does as I tell her, and I groan as my sensitive tip glides over her tongue and into her mouth. She closes her lips around my shaft and relaxes as I slide in and out.

Fuck *me*, she looks hot. Her eyes seem almost golden today, and she's looking straight at my face as she sucks me. I realize her hands are behind her, crossed at her lower back.

There are things Dani doesn't know about herself, but *I'm* just starting to figure her out.

I move my hands to her head, digging my fingers into her hair. I gather it into one hand and grasp my cock with the other. Holding her head still, I push myself deeper, feeling a rush of pleasure each time I hit the back of her throat.

Gotta stop or I'm gonna come all over her. And she needs to get hers first.

I pull my cock from Dani's mouth, and she gasps.

She looks glorious. Her lipstick is smeared across her face, her eyes are streaming, and her mascara streaks her face like war paint.

She laughs. There's a manic edge to it.

"*Please* make me come," she says, wiping her eyes with the back of her hand. "You're killing me. I swear I never got this turned on with anyone else."

She lies back and spreads her legs for me, and I can see she's not joking. Her pussy is puffy, the lips a deep rosy hue, and her clit is so swollen that I wonder if it might be too sensitive for me to touch. Her wetness is everywhere - on her thighs, on the seat, running into the crack of her ass.

I retake my previous position, my face inches from her pussy. I breathe on her, and she moans wretchedly, reaching for my head so she can push me closer.

"No," I say. "You're not running the show. Put your hands up and hold onto the seat."

I expected some dissent, but Dani isn't prepared to do anything that might slow me down. Her hands are above her head in a flash, and I go to work.

She tastes incredible. Clean and fresh, with a tang that's unique to her. I run the flat of my tongue from her asshole to her clit, and lap at the swollen button, circling it slowly.

Dani exhales slowly, ending with a strangled cry as I slip a finger into her pussy.

"You're so fucking juicy," I say as I work it back and forth. "You ever get this wet for anyone else?"

"No," she gasps.

"And what about this?" I rub my thumb over her clit, enjoying the feel of her tensing around my finger. "Who else ever made you feel this good, huh?"

"No one." She arches her back as I flick my tongue over her clit again, finding a rhythm as I finger-fuck her. "Only you."

I stop moving my hand, my finger still buried inside her. I move my lips over her twitching folds, but I know it's not enough.

Dani moves her arms so she can sit up on her elbows. She looks down at me.

"What?" she pants. "Why did you stop?"

I lap her clit, enjoying the sight as her eyes roll.

"Because you mentioned someone else. I don't like it." I reach up and pinch her nipple. "*Is* there someone else, Dani?"

She's trying to scowl at me, but her eyes give away her desperation.

This woman wants me to make her come, but I'm gonna make her say it.

"There's no one else!" she cries. "Kal, for fuck's sake. There *should* be someone else. *Anyone* else would make more sense."

I add a second finger and begin to move.

"Eyes on me and keep talking. Convince me."

Dani wants to hate me. If looks could kill, I'd be a corpse. But her hips missed a memo, and they're pushing against my hand.

She wants to fight me, and I adore her for that, but now isn't the time.

"Ever since the night we spent together, I've thought about you all the fucking time. When I touch myself, I see *you*."

I step up the pace, moving my tongue over her clit faster.

"I know you're no good," she whimpers, "and there's no future for this - for *us*. But I want you anyway."

My cock throbs at her words. "That's my good girl," I say, squeezing her thigh. "You come for me now."

I feel Dani's pussy spasming, clutching my fingers so tightly that I can't pull away. Her pleasure soaks my face, and she cries out, gripping the seat.

I'm inside her before she has the chance to come down from her orgasm, and she clutches my back as I pump my hips. She's breathing heavily in my ear, and I push up onto my hands to look at her face while I fuck her.

Her eyes are narrow, the lids heavy. She places her hands on my chest, digging her nails into me.

I take her slender neck in my hand, gripping her but not too hard. She closes her eyes and gasps but makes no protest, and I feel my climax building.

"You're mine," I say, slamming her harder. "I'm gonna show you."

I pull out of Dani's grasping pussy and grab my cock with my free hand, the other still around her throat. I pull her upright, the head of my cock right by her face.

She opens her mouth and tilts her head back, ready to take it.

"You're such a pretty little slut," I growl, pumping my hand along my shaft. "You want my come all over you? Marking your body, making you mine?" I rub the tip along her lips, and she moans, licking the salty wetness from me.

"Come on my face," she says. "I want it."

I grunt as my climax smashes through my body, enjoying the view as streams of come coat Dani's lips. My seed runs down her chin, and she leans back, letting it stream over her collarbone and onto her tits.

"Fuck," I say, trying to calm my breathing. "That was hot. And kinda out of nowhere."

Dani isn't making much effort to clean herself up. She skips the bra and stuffs it into her bag, pulling her clothes back on even as my come is drying on her skin.

We're dressed and vaguely respectable again. I turn on the car engine, and we sit for a moment in silence as the windows de-mist.

Dani is avoiding my eyes. She's sitting in the front passenger seat beside me, with her legs curled up and her knees tipped towards the door.

"Home?" I ask.

"Yeah. I have somewhere to be tonight."

I glance at her. "That means *I* have somewhere to be, too. Where?"

"The Samhain Ball."

"Ah, yes. I go every year. "

Dani frowns at me. "I never saw you there."

I smile and give a non-commital shrug but say nothing.

Somehow I doubt that Danica Pushkin has ever attended the *real* Samhain Ball.

But I said I would teach her things, and something tells me she's more than ready to learn.

I put the car into gear and pull out of the lot.

Just wait, Dani. You ain't seen nothing yet.

13

KAL

Brutus is stuck like glue to Fyodor. Every minute of the day, he seems to be there, and I get the feeling the guy would love a reason to fuck me up, so my bloody vengeance has been forced to take a back seat.

I have to concede that Fyodor isn't as stupid as I thought. Idina waxed lyrical for hours about her hated brother-in-law's poor judgment and weak-minded morals, but I'm not seeing it. I thought I could connive my way into his home and murder him with little trouble, but I've been observing him, and there are things I definitely didn't know.

Fyodor has a stoic gravitas that influences everyone around him. He talks to his people behind closed doors, and they do his bidding. The man never doubts and doesn't expect the worst in others.

And he's *besotted* with his girls.

I'm waiting for Dani. She's been getting ready for an hour, and the rest of the Pushkins have already left.

I head into the lounge and refresh my vodka.

I gotta slow down. It's my third drink, and I need to keep a level head for what I've got planned tonight.

I think about the scene in this room only an hour ago.

When I came in, Dani and her mother were eating *vareniki* - Russian dumplings - with sour cream, and Fyodor was reading papers. I tried to keep out of things by sitting in an armchair and laughing at Marta's jokes.

Dani cleared her plate and put it down. Her father looked at her over his paper.

"You done?" he asked.

I tensed up, waiting for the argument to start. Maybe he thought Dani had overeaten - this was always Idina's favorite shitty little jibe whenever she felt like bringing Vera down. Or perhaps he got pissed off about something else, and she was in trouble for not reading his mind...

"It's ok, Papa," Dani said. "You're busy. I'll get more myself."

"*Nyet, dorogayay,*" Fyodor said. He stood and walked out of the room, pausing to squeeze Dani's shoulder as he passed.

In a minute, he was back with a fresh plate of dumplings. He handed it to Dani, and she laughed when she saw what he'd done.

"Papa! I'm going to be twenty-one in a few days! When will you decide I'm too old for this?"

I looked to see that Fyodor had arranged the dumplings into a face. Two eyes, a nose, and a mouth. A heap of sour cream and chopped chives made a beard.

Fyodor just smiled at her. "I'll stop doing it when it doesn't make you smile like that anymore."

Marta chuckled, looking at her husband and rolling her eyes. He grinned and shrugged.

I was dumbfounded. Still am.

What the fuck kind of family is this?

My family doesn't go in for little games and affectionate gestures. We know things about each other, sure, but we keep that information in the memory vault, ready to pull it out when we want to hurt one another. My mother's catalog of misused knowledge is so vast that it makes the Smithsonian look like a small-town library.

And Erik. My stepfather never shared a joke with me in his life. The only thing he ever found funny was when he roped me into his creative punishments. He would have me choose between me punching my brother or him doing it. I always preferred to be the one to hit Simeon because Erik would hit *much* harder.

But Erik always thought it was a hoot to watch.

"Hey."

I turn to see Dani in the doorway. She gives a little twirl, and my breath catches in my throat.

Her burgundy velvet dress kisses the ground, split to mid-thigh. The high halter neck contrasts with the plunge in the back, and her hair is piled up in her head in an artfully messy jumble of curls.

She looks incredible and very much the part. She pops her hip like a model, then frowns.

"You don't like it?" she asks.

I realize I'm not saying anything. "Sorry, *milaya*. Of course I like it. Well worth the wait."

She claps her hands. "So hurry up then! You're already drinking, and I want to have fun!

∼

The Samhain Ball has two faces.

On the one hand, it's a party for powerful, wealthy, and shady people. Politicians, police, judges, businessmen, millionaires, and criminals spend the evening back-slapping and hand-shaking, congratulating one another on being masters of the universe. This is the event that Dani has attended in the past, the one she thinks she's going to tonight.

The *other* Samhain Ball is upstairs.

The hotel's top floor is closed, and the elevator is guarded. There are no invitations or requirements other than a lot of money if you want to make the list. But once you get up there, you're no one. You're anonymous, and only your actions can define you.

No phones. No names. No aftermath.

One night to let it all out.

We don't attract any attention as we get out of the car. The hotel lobby is full of people milling around, checking in their coats and air-kissing.

Then I see him.

Fuck.

Simeon is here. *Why?* There can only be one answer.

I scan the room. I need to send Dani away so I can get rid of my idiot brother before this whole situation blows up in my face. Mercifully, I see Mel in the cloakroom queue, struggling under several coats.

"Your sister is over there. Help her, then join the party. There's something I gotta do." I move away quickly before Dani asks any troublesome questions.

Simeon is sitting at a table in the bar area, waving jauntily in my direction.

"What the fuck do you want?" I say, sitting down beside him. "You know why I'm here. Can't you let me have my fun?"

"You're not supposed to be enjoying yourself," Simeon sneers. "You've had plenty of time to get the job done, but I saw Fyodor Pushkin just now, alive and well. Idina won't be happy."

"I spoke to her earlier, and she knows I'm playing the long game. Don't pretend you're here because she asked you to be. You're just spying on me, hoping I'll fuck up so you can tell on me to Mommy and get a pat on the head."

Simeon sniffs and adjusts his shirt collar. "So what is if I am? It's only me who seems to know that my father was wrong about you. *He* was strong. You don't have the guts to take what's ours."

I don't want to hurt Simeon. I've already hurt him enough to last a lifetime. But he's pushing my buttons because he knows exactly what I'm afraid of.

There will be time to deal with all this bullshit, but tonight is for us - me and Dani. I'm already buzzed on vodka and ready to do my thing, and this little weasel and his sad machinations are not gonna kill my good vibes.

Still, the urge to slap the smirk off Simeon's face is strong.

"Fucking *leave*," I say. "You can't get in upstairs anyway because you don't get enough allowance. I have money to burn."

"*My* father's money," he says. "Mine, by right."

"But not by his Will. He didn't leave you a thing. So go home. It's past your bedtime."

I leave Simeon to stew and head off to retrieve Dani from the party. I find her at the buffet table, dipping strawberries into the chocolate fountain.

"Doesn't your Papa make these into faces for you, too?"

Dani raises her eyebrow. "You dick. How would you like it if I laughed at your family traditions?"

"We don't have any except bitterness and grudges. What's the point?"

Dani stares at me. I don't like her expression - confusion with a tinge of pity. "That sounds bleak, Kal. But it's not a surprise, knowing what I know about your father."

"Stepfather."

The distinction feels ever more important. The vision I hold in my mind of Erik is folding in on itself, morphing into something new. I want to ask her what she means, but I resist, pulling my thoughts back into the room.

Not now. Nothing is taking this night away from me.

I grab Dani's hand and pull her out of the ballroom. We hang a right into a short corridor leading to the elevator that will take us both just as high as we need to go.

"Where are we going?" Dani hisses. "We can't just leave the party!"

"We'll be back. We have another engagement to attend."

The guy guarding the elevator is an old friend, Lev. I give him a nod, but now's not the time for small talk. I take out my phone, pull up the QR code on the screen, and he scans it.

"Password?" he asks.

"Mine is 'blackout.'"

Lev presses a button on the wall, and the elevator doors slide open with a whisper. We step inside, and he leans in to push the floor number.

"See you on the other side," he says.

Dani says nothing as we walk down the corridor. The room doors are all numbered, and room one has an additional label. It says 'preparation.'

I get a rush when I see the masks. Every year it gets to me, and this time the feeling is amplified by the knowledge that I'm gonna be kicking it up a notch.

Dani gasps, taking in the rows of disguises.

Clown, plague doctor, jester, devil, fairy, and so many others. Some plain, some adorned with jewels and precious metals.

A young woman sits on a chair beside the masks, and I smile to see Dani gawking at her. The girl is wearing a rubber skirt with a matching corset. Her mask is also rubber and covers her eyes. The bunny ears extending from the top of the mask are a foot high.

"Choose. I'll make a note of it."

"What is this?" Dani whispers.

I turn to her and smile. "You're about to find out."

The girl in the bunny mask laughs and wags a finger at Dani.

"Woooo," she says. "You are *lucky*, sweetie. I'd let this tall drink o'water do *anything* he wanted to *me*."

"Fuck off," Dani snarls at her, and that's it.

I wanna get into the action.

I choose a green mask covered in golden leaves. Dani runs her hands along the shelf, selecting a black lace design that makes her look like a superhero.

As we secure the masks on our faces, bunny girl gives us the brief.

"No identification, okay? As far as anyone else is concerned, you're ghosts. Each room has a safeword on the wall - know it before you begin. Anyone who disregards a safeword will get the shit kicked out of them and barred for life *at best*. Questions?"

Dani looks at me. I reckon she probably has a few.

"No," I say.

"Leave your cell phones," bunny girl says, pointing at the small lockers stacked up against the opposite wall. Dani hands me her phone without a word.

My phone rings as I go to put it in the locker. I frown at the caller ID.

Idina. I swipe to red, slamming the locker closed and pocketing the key.

"Come on," I say, taking Dani's hand. "You're safe with me, I promise."

"I hope not," she replies, "but I really wanna find out for sure."

As I look at her, a coy little tendril of feeling wraps around my cold heart. It scares me.

I don't get her. This curious, spirited, creative woman is everything I'm not. But her warmth is getting to me, melting places within that have been frozen solid for years.

I'm seeing things differently.

I always thought my future was already written. Vengeance. Bloodshed. A legacy denied, taken by force. Honor restored.

But that story has no safe place for Dani, and when I think about the differences between her life and mine, I can't reconcile them.

The words in my book are sliding off the page, rearranging, realigning. The noble tale of a displaced king is re-writing itself into a brutal, toxic family tragedy, with the Pushkins the wronged party.

Maybe I'm going crazy. Maybe I am weak.

But right now, Dani is all I can see. In this place, I will *truly* get to know her.

14

DANI

As Kal's hand settles on the door handle, my heart runs a mile a minute.

"In this room are the people who like to watch," Kal says. His hand grips mine. "There are also those who like to perform. But observers cannot touch anyone in the red zone, so don't worry."

"I'm scared, Kal," I whisper.

"Good," he says. "You can't reach the heights without that. And believe me, I'm gonna take you there."

He pushes open the door.

The room is enormous. It looks like the library in a gothic castle. The walls are lined with bookshelves, and tables and chairs are laid out as though it's a cabaret. There's a bar, but it's table service - staff glide discreetly around the room, serving drinks.

In the middle of the room is a square of crimson carpet, and in the center is a gymnastics horse. A woman bends over it, her wrists tied to the handgrips. Apart from a harlequin mask, she's completely naked.

Kal stands behind me, his arm around my waist. He pulls me to him, and I feel his stiffening cock against my ass.

"Oh, this turns you on?" I say.

Kal's other hand strokes up my flank and cups my breast, his thumb brushing my nipple.

"Yes, it does," he says, "but not as much as your reaction. Do you even know what this is doing to *you*, Dani?"

I both love and hate how in tune Kal is with me. I didn't realize my mouth was hanging open, my core heating at the sight before me, but he did.

A man is standing behind the bound woman. He's fully dressed, a plain black mask obscuring his features, and he's holding something in his hand.

I pull away from Kal's embrace and move closer, sliding onto a small couch at the edge of the carpeted area. Kal settles beside me, his erection evident. A glance around the room tells me he's not the only one getting off on this little show.

On closer examination, the man is holding a butt plug. It's shaped like a pine cone, lightly textured in forest-green glass. He steps closer to the woman and parts the cheeks of her ass with one hand, exposing her rosy asshole to everyone.

Without warning, he spits on her, rubbing the butt plug over her tiny hole. She moans, her hair hanging as she moves her head from side to side.

I'm transfixed. I've seen nothing like this in my life. My wetness is pooling in my folds, and I'm worried it'll go through the dress because I made the rash decision not to wear any panties. They were spoiling the line of my outfit.

The man pushes the plug into the woman's ass, and she cries out as it stretches her. Some of the audience move closer, trying to get a better look. I'm sitting on the edge of the couch, barely conscious of my movements as I grind my pussy against the upholstery.

"You dirty bitch," Kal murmurs, and I break out of my reverie long enough to look at him. I thought he was talking about the bound woman, but as I meet his eyes, I realize he meant me.

I want to keep my expression neutral, but I can't. He's sitting back, his arms draped along the top of the couch like he's a king, and this is his court. The scene could be playing out just for us despite all the other people in the room.

I tear my eyes away from his, drawn by the cries from the red carpet.

The man is working the plug in and out of the woman's asshole. She's enjoying the room's attention, making eye contact with the audience as her partner plays with her.

I feel a surge of jealousy.

I want to be the one everyone is looking at. I want every woman here to watch Kal, wishing he was touching her, fucking her, but knowing he's off limits. Because he's *mine*.

The man frees his cock from his pants and eases it into the woman's pussy, leaving the plug buried in her ass. She hisses through her teeth as he grabs her ass with both hands, pulling out of her again.

A crack rings out like a gunshot. The man massages the place where his hand landed, a reddish bloom rushing to the woman's skin. He plunges back inside her as he spanks her again.

Crack.

In my peripheral vision, I see Kal move. He's kneeling on the ground. I'm dimly aware of him lying on the floor, his face upside down between my feet.

Crack.

Kal tugs at my dress.

"Down here, Dani. You keep watching, and I'll make you come."

Crack.

The woman is losing it, her cries getting more ragged and desperate as her partner fucks her harder. Kal pulls my dress again, and I look at him.

"You wanted me to keep touching you last night, right? Sit on my face, and I'll make it up to you."

He's a demon.

Does he know what I fucking dreamed about? How?

Of course he doesn't. He got into my room. It really happened.

I decide I don't care. He's right - he owes me, leaving me wet and wanting in the middle of the night like that...

I slide onto my knees, my dress over Kal's head. He slips his hands over my thighs as I straddle his face, a muffled moan escaping him.

"Oh fuck," he says.

I sigh as his tongue spears my soaking pussy, lapping up my juice. His stubble grazes my clit, and he maneuvers me so he can suck it gently.

I'm shaking. I didn't realize how little it would take to make me come, but it's building already. Kal's tongue works my clit insistently, dipping into my pussy now and again, and the pleasure sends bolts of electricity up my spine. As his mouth works its magic, I brace my back against the couch for support.

The bound woman's eyes are closed, but as her partner spanks her one last time, her orgasm hits her, and she opens her eyes, looking straight into mine. Her cry of ecstasy spurs Kal on, and he lashes his tongue over my clit, pushing me over the edge.

He holds my waist tightly as I come, gushing wetness over his face. As I come down from the peak, I notice that I have an audience of my own. So many men are looking at me.

I've never known a thrill like it. I feel like a goddess, a siren.

The couple on the carpet is done. The man is untying the woman, rubbing her wrists tenderly as she smiles at him.

Kal pushes at my thighs, lifting my ass off my heels and resting me on the edge of the couch. He rubs his face as he stands.

"I nearly drowned," he grins, "but it was worth it."

I stare at him, words failing me. Someone speaks up, breaking the spell.

"I think you guys had better take the floor."

The man is helping his partner into a satin robe. He gestures at the red carpet.

Kal holds out a hand to me. He leads me to the red carpet, my legs still shaking.

I want more of this feeling. Something about the masks makes it all seem dreamlike.

All those eyes on me. On *us*.

Kal pushes me to my knees and walks away. I'm still too dazed to fully take in what's going on, but I can see him rummaging in an oversized ottoman standing at the edge of the carpeted area.

A moment later, he's back. He gets onto one knee and takes my chin in his hand, turning my face to the back wall.

Above the balcony doors are letters a foot high, scrawled in red paint. The word is 'lamplight.'

"That's the safe word, Dani," Kal says. "I'll confess, I don't want to hear it. But if you do say it, I'll stop. Otherwise, your consent is assumed. Understand?"

I nod.

Kal stands and moves quickly behind me. He's shifting my limbs, securing my wrists and ankles to a wooden board.

"It's a pillory," he whispers. "Sometimes called 'stocks,' but this one has four holes and holds your feet in between your hands."

He's not wrong. I'm stuck in this position, my hands behind me.

Kal stands before me again, his cock making an obscene tent in his pants, just inches from my face. He undoes his zipper, and his cock springs free, looking larger than ever. It's been hard for so long now. It must be painful.

I open my mouth and watch as he grasps his erection at the base, sighing as I run my tongue around the tip. He pushes into my mouth, and I relax my throat, doing my best to take him as deep as he wants. I gag a little, and he growls with delight as he pulls his cock free.

"Spit on it," he says.

I work my throat, pulling up as much saliva as I can, and he rests his cock on my lips as I spit. I watch as it runs down his shaft, and he pumps his hand up and down, moving the saliva along the length. His other hand reaches behind my neck, undoing the button holding up my halter-neck.

There's a ripple of appreciation in the room as my dress falls to my waist, exposing my breasts. Kal pushes back into my mouth again, holding my head in place with both hands as he fucks my face.

The room is a blur, but the audience is entranced. Some men are openly jerking off. Others have wandered off into their own filthy little worlds, fucking on the furniture.

So many people watching me as Kal uses my mouth. I never dreamed this could feel so good…

Kal cries out and yanks his twitching cock from between my lips, catching it in his fist. He pumps it vigorously, his come landing on my face in hot silky ribbons.

A few people launch into spontaneous applause.

Kal is breathing heavily. He helps me to my feet, and I burst into laughter as a server appears at my side, silently holding a warm washcloth.

"What service," I say, wiping my face. Kal has already zipped up, and he rearranges the front of my dress, restoring my modesty.

"So did you mean to come on my face, or…"

"I didn't have time to decide," he says. "It just happened. But you look fucking gorgeous like that."

I move off the red carpet and sit in an armchair, closing my eyes while I recover.

Kal turns away from me for a second, and it's enough.

Hands on my head, thumbs boring into my temples, gripping my skull like a vice. I'm being dragged forwards, my neck jangling with pain, and I fall off the chair onto my knees. The hands holding me prevent me from moving any further.

A stranger is pushing his cock toward my mouth.

He smells of jock sweat and cheap cologne, and I clamp my mouth shut, trying to grab his wrists and push his hands off me. He lets go of my head and grabs a handful of my hair with one hand. With the other, he pinches my nose, holding my nostrils closed.

It's all happening so quickly. I twist my body, trying to free myself, but it's no use.

"Open your mouth, your fuckin' whore," the man snarls.

Kal fills the room with a primal roar of rage. He's behind my attacker, wrapping his arm around his neck. The man squawks in shock and lets go of me, and I scurry backward along the floor, crashing into the table.

Kal has the man in a chokehold, pushing him in front of him. He's a foot taller than my attacker, and the man can't get any purchase, his toes barely touching the floor. Kal spits curses in his ear as he shoves him along.

"You fucking filthy bastard fucking cunt…"

They are heading out onto the balcony.

No one moves or tries to intervene. There's an air of passive acceptance like this is natural justice. The way of things.

Kal won't do it. He's just scaring him. He's—

A firm shove between the shoulder blades, and the man topples over the rail, disappearing from view. Kal stands there as though he's taking in the view.

There's a sickening crunch, and outside, someone screams.

Kal turns around and walks back inside, closing the balcony door. He picks me up and holds me tightly to him as we head for the door.

"Time to go," he says. The pain is audible in his voice. "I'm sorry, *milaya*. I'm so sorry."

Some of the rooms are given over for aftercare. They're much like any deluxe hotel room, with good bathrooms and spa facilities.

I sit on the edge of the bed in silence. Kal palms my neck, tilting my head gently.

"Tell me if it hurts," he says. "I don't think *I* did anything, but that fucking pig—"

"It's fine. Really. I'm not hurt, and nothing really happened."

Kal's eyes darken. "I said you'd be safe with me," he says. "I never saw something like that happen before. If I thought someone would assault you, I'd never have brought you here."

He looks stricken with guilt, his eyes searching mine, and I feel something stir. A possibility that never occurred to me before.

Kal is typical Bratva. Possessive, arrogant, commanding. But maybe he isn't a total asshole after all.

Most of the time, he's relaxed, cynical, and sardonic. Qualities I actually appreciate, despite his tendency to tease me.

But Kal has absolutely no chill regarding me and my safety. He just completely fucked up that man and he neither knows nor cares whether he's dead. He doesn't give a shit about the consequences. Instead, he's here by my side, concerned only with me.

It doesn't feel like he's suffocating me. Instead, I feel cherished, even adored, and it's unexpected.

I've never wanted the mafia life to swallow me. No good will come of it. But Kal Antonov is the man who left his twisted family behind and came to us begging for a chance. And so far, he hasn't put a foot wrong.

He's choosing to change. Maybe I can do the same.

15

KAL

Fyodor and I are alone.

It's the opportunity I've been looking for. Brutus isn't here, and no one else is up yet. The Pushkin patriarch is taking his morning constitutional and asked me along.

I could choke the life out of him and leave him on the cold gravel, his head in the jasmine. Leave Dani and her mother to find him. I'd make a few calls, issue a few threats, pay a few people, and that would be that.

The Pushkins would be suddenly and wholly frozen out, and I'd take the empire my stepfather had failed to seize. Easy.

But seismic shifts are taking place inside me. I can't imagine Fyodor coming to such an ignoble end. He deserves better than that.

"You seem distracted," Fyodor says. "Here's a question to focus your mind on, Kal. Have you ever wondered why it was so easy for you to walk into our lives like this?"

Yes, as a matter of fact. It seems painfully naïve for a Pakhan to open his home to me, a sworn enemy, and entrust his precious daughter into my care...

"I just assumed you believed me when I said I've abandoned my family," I say. "Why? *Don't* you believe me?"

"No," Fyodor says, "I don't, not entirely. But Marta thinks you're considering it, and my wife is a smart woman." He stops and frowns at the rose bushes. "These need cutting back. But seriously - I'm not living up to the hype, am I?"

"My mother gave me a different impression of you," I say, glancing at him warily.

He doesn't seem to be armed. *Where is he going with this?*

"As you know, you and I are not related," Fyodor continues. "Your stepfather, my brother, was nothing to me. Our parents did everything possible to make Erik hate me, and I was their favorite. When Erik grew up, he found a woman with the same twisted, bitter outlook as our mother. Two of a kind, they were."

I have heard none of this before. Luckily, Fyodor is in the mood to lay it all out.

"Even though Erik was older, my father made it known that I was to become Pakhan. When he died, I cleaned up much of the operation here, and Idina didn't like it. She pushed Erik to pressure me into people trafficking, but I have my limits, and it became a sore point."

Sounds exactly like her - no thought for anyone's essential humanity. Just treat them like commodities because why not, right?

"Erik and Idina distanced themselves. Before you were a year old, they said they were through with us all, and Erik changed his name to Antonov. I never even met your brother and sister." Fyodor sighs and looks at the ground. "Then one day, years later, Erik was back, a rag-tag group of street scum backing him. He tried to take the Pushkin empire by force, but he didn't have a plan, and all his goons soon split when they saw we had them on the run. I tried to talk him down, but he kept trying to fight, and he lost his shit and tried to shoot Mel. She was just a kid at the time."

Fuck. In all the times Idina sat me down and told me the story of Erik's glorious martyrdom, she never told me he tried to kill a *child*.

Fyodor could be lying, but the shine in his eyes tells me otherwise.

These are memories. Bullshit doesn't make grown men cry.

"My mother told me you killed Erik. Is it true?"

"Yes." Fyodor's voice is heavy with regret. "I shot him before he could murder my daughter. And not a day passes that I don't wish it could all have been different, Kal. Erik could have made better choices. He didn't have to destroy himself to prove he was worth something."

My head hurts.

This information is mostly the same as what I've been told my whole life - that Fyodor murdered Erik in cold blood, denying him his rightful place as leader of the Pushkin Bratva. But Idina only showed me some of the picture, and with Fyodor's lines and colors added, the image is not the one I had in my mind.

My mother made me believe in destiny, and I hung every scrap of my self-worth on achieving it. I don't know who I am if I'm not the man she wants me to be.

I thought I wanted to be that man, too. But the facade is crumbling away, and I don't know what's behind it.

Maybe this legacy doesn't have to define me.

But what will I stand for instead?

Dani.

A man tried to assault her, and I threw him off a balcony. I hope the cunt is dead. I regret nothing, and I'd do it again for far less.

Despite her fear, she allowed me to pull her into my dark world of sensual pleasures without a backward glance. I never thought I could express my dominant urges with someone I care about, and it's a revelation.

Now that I've spent some time with this family, my own looks more rotten than ever. And Fyodor has given me a glimpse of a toxic chain of dysfunction that has been ruining lives for generations.

I don't have to be Erik. I could choose to be *myself*. But who the fuck *am* I?

Fyodor sees the turmoil on my face and places a hand on my shoulder.

"You're here because you're the best chance we have of bringing this sad saga to a close, one way or another." He nods at the house. "This is my family home, and it's full of ghosts. You were right when you said we were all Pushkins once. You're not my blood, but you're not Erik's either."

I look at the Pushkin mansion, trying to imagine Erik and Fyodor as boys. I feel a surge of empathy for them both.

They were innocent children, and their parents let them down. Fyodor didn't repeat the cycle with his own family, but Erik and Idina reveled in having the power to inflict pain rather than suffer it. A thread of common experience binds Fyodor and me in a way I could never have anticipated.

Simeon, Vera, and I are just frightened, abused little kids inside. The contrast between us and the Pushkins burns me, but I'm no longer angry. Just tired.

I watch as Fyodor walks up the steps and through the front door. He turns back in the doorway to speak to me again.

"Your choices are not easy, kid. I understand, believe me."

"My mother always told me blood is thicker than water," I reply. "Idina is my family. She and my siblings are all I've got."

"That's a misquote," Fyodor says. "'The full expression is 'the blood of the covenant is thicker than the water of the womb.' It means that the bonds you choose in life are worth more than the circumstantial ones. You don't *choose* who your relatives are, but *family*? That *is* a choice. Be wise."

As the door closes on Fyodor Pushkin, the door in my mind slams too.

I can't do it.

Fuck knows what will happen now, but Fyodor Pushkin will not die at my hands. My mother was wrong, and I won't be her creature anymore.

Four calls from Idina now since last night, and I've ignored them all. I take out my phone and send her a message.

Situation tense and not as expected. Handling it. Stand by.

Suitably vague. Hopefully, that'll shut her up for now. But I can't stall forever.

∼

Dani is in the outhouse, mixing paint. She's wearing overalls, her hair in a scarf. When she sees me, she stops stirring, resting the piece of wood across the top of the paint can.

"*You* are the fucking devil," she says, jabbing a finger at me. "I can't believe you made me go back into the ball downstairs and act natural!"

"You said yourself that we couldn't just vanish for the night. Besides, I thought you liked the chocolate fountain?"

"And what the fuck, Kal?" Dani asks, ignoring my remark. "You sneaked into my room and touched my pussy while I was asleep?"

"You weren't asleep, though, were you? And you didn't stop me, so..." I shrug.

"That makes it okay, does it? How did you even know the door code?"

"I remembered your birthday from your passport and tried it. I was delighted to find out how predictable you are."

Dani steps towards me, and I can't help but move to meet her. Something about her pulls at me. She trails her fingertip into the hollow of my throat.

"Couldn't keep away from me. Even though it was dangerous, you had to do it. Right?"

This woman knows that I have rough edges. She knows I have it in me to be a really fucking bad guy - I killed for her last night. But she doesn't just accept it.

She craves the darkness in me. It makes her brightness more vivid, just as she makes me relax and lean into the freak I want to be.

I used to haunt her nightmares. Now I'm the monster in her bed, not the monster under it, and I'll slaughter anyone who so much as offends her from here on out.

16

DANI

It's my birthday, and Kal has a surprise for me.

The first surprise is that my father is letting him take me out. There's no pretense that Kal is on minder's duties - he's taking me on a date, and my Mama and Papa are allowing it.

An Antonov has permission to escort me, the youngest Pushkin daughter, out on the town. Scandalous.

Of course, my Papa knows nothing of Kal's less-than-professional conduct. As bodyguards go, Kal makes Kevin Costner look like a eunuch. Whitney Houston would have found a whole new octave with my man's methods…

Is Kal my man? We haven't put a name to it. But over the last few days, something changed.

We're still snatching opportunities to get our freak on. But my door is locked at night, and I changed the passcode. I don't want Kal to come to me when there's a possibility of my father catching us because I'm not sure that he wouldn't just blow Kal's head off with the rifle he keeps under his bed.

I'm almost ready to go. I hear Mama downstairs, trying to convince Kal to eat some of my birthday cake. He's insisting he doesn't like sweet stuff, but my mother is having none of it, and Mel finds the whole thing hilarious. Her hooting laughter rings through the house.

My Papa is out. It's one of the rare evenings when he has to deal with something himself, and I hate it.

We all get twitchy and scared, worrying Mama will get the call. The one to tell us Papa is dead at the hands of some double-crossing asshole. The fear is always there that someone will take Papa's honor and trust, only to weaponize it and hurt him in some unspeakable way.

I put in my earrings, and I'm ready.

∽

Kal gives a low whistle as I walk into the kitchen. Mel punches him in the arm.

"Mikhail, behave!" she says. "You look wonderful, Dani. Too good for the likes of him, that's for sure."

Kal rolls his eyes and takes my hand. "With that, I think we'll get going," he says. He grins at my mother. "So you're sure Fyodor isn't waiting by the gate, ready to shoot the tires as I drive by?"

"He wouldn't do something like that," Mama says mischievously. "He loves the Alfa and wouldn't risk damaging it. He'd just kneecap you before you got in."

Mel snorts into her drink, coughing as the liquid goes up her nose. I giggle as she wheezes with laughter.

Kal winces. "I hope you're kidding, but I'm not sure enough. It's worth the risk, though."

He grins at me, and I grin back.

On the night of the Samhain Ball, I saw several facets of Kal Antonov.

There's still more I don't know about Kal, but I like him.

God help me. I *really* fucking like him.

I *could* love him. It seems possible.

When I met him, he was just a horny, sexy bastard. Then I discovered who he was, and I didn't think he was capable of complexity. I couldn't see him as anything more than a messed-up, malignant force of nature.

I was wrong. He's more than that.

And he will bring the whole world to its knees before he sees me suffer. I'm safe with him. We all are.

∼

"Is it a play you've seen before?" I ask.

"No. I don't know anything about it."

"Then what makes you think it's a good birthday surprise?"

"I'm confident."

I slip off my shoes, my silk jumpsuit sliding along the smooth fabric, and I put my feet up.

Kal won't tell me what play we're going to see.

When we arrived at the East Village theater, he led me through a side door and into the VIP area. A word in an usher's ear, and we were seated in a private box. A wedge of hundred-dollar bills didn't hurt, either.

There's a couch and also a velvet chaise. We can summon our usher with a mute button if we need anything.

I sit on the chaise, watching the stragglers take their seats in the stands below.

"I think you don't give a shit about the play, and you just want to fuck me here in public."

He raises his eyebrows at me. "You said it, *milaya,* not me. But if the play is boring, I'll take you up on it."

The house lights go down. The commotion in the room fades to silence.

A greenish light begins to rise at the back of the stage, and a projection appears on the stage wall as it grows brighter. It's a young man writing.

His voice echoes as he speaks.

"3 May. Bistritz. Left Munich at 8.35 pm, on 1 May, arriving at Vienna early next morning..."

I leap to my feet, grabbing the balustrade to see better.

It's *Dracula*.

Time and space stand still as I watch the classic tale unfold. Literature's most famous vampire is a source of endless fascination to me, and this retelling is full of symbolism and Gothic atmosphere.

When the curtain falls for the last time, I'm in tears. I realize I didn't speak to Kal once. It's not until we are walking to the car that I remember what he said.

"You must have enjoyed that," I say, "because you didn't try and do anything inappropriate to me for the whole time we were in there."

I shiver. It's a cold night, and my outfit is classy but not exactly warm. Kal removes his jacket, wrapping it around my shoulders.

"I think it'll stay with me," he says, "but I wouldn't have distracted you for anything. I'm not sure I can hold a candle to Dracula. What's your attraction to him?"

"I guess he's a classic Byronic lead, much like you."

He frowns. "What the fuck does *that* mean?"

"A brooding, difficult hero with a dark past and raging, powerful passions. That's you all over."

We're at the parking lot. Kal takes out the car keys and unlocks the car, opening the passenger door for me. I slide onto the seat, and he gets into the driver's side.

"That is *not* an accurate description of me," he says sternly, starting the engine.

"Yes, it is. What part of that isn't true?"

He cocks his head for a moment, glancing my way.

"I'm not a hero," he grins, "but the rest is right on the money."

I laugh. "I'll tell you something else you have in common with Dracula."

"Excellent dress sense?" Kal drums his fingers on the steering wheel. "A preference for a full-bodied red with dinner?"

"No. You're both absolute Counts."

Kal laughs. He keeps one hand on the wheel and reaches for me with the other. His hand rests on my knee, sliding up to squeeze my thigh.

"Very funny. But a Count?" he says, scoffing at the thought. "Fuck that. You and me? We're *royalty*."

∽

I don't want to go home. I'm still on a high after the play and am not ready to return to reality. So when Kal turns off towards the ferry port, I'm surprised but intrigued.

"Don't you wanna know where we're going?" Kal asks.

"Of course I do. But I figure I'm gonna find out either way, so why ask?" I wave my hands in the air. "Weave your magic for me."

No one but me ever sees the smile he's wearing now. Brooding and moody, he may be, but *I* can crack that tough exterior every time.

We park near the Lower Manhattan ferry port, and Kal leads me to the quayside. He stops beside a speedboat, and I gesture at my heels.

"I can't climb in there, not in these shoes. I'll go over the side."

"I will throw you in there myself if you don't move your ass." Kal jumps off the deck into the boat. "Come on. I'll catch you."

I don't want to jump. I'm scared I'll turn an ankle.

"Dani." He reaches up to me.

I hesitate for too long, and Kal takes hold of the mooring rope, using it to hoist himself up and out. Without a word, he grabs me by the waist and chucks me onto his shoulder.

"*No*, Kal, don't do it!"

Of course, he ignores my protests and leaps onto the boat. It rocks with the impact, water sloshing up the sides, and he waits a moment for it to settle before placing me on my feet.

"Sit down and relax. We'll be there in just a few minutes."

∽

Governors Island. I've lived in New York for years and never visited it. Kal ties up the boat and helps me ashore.

We walk along a path through a park, bronze-colored leaves tumbling around us. The lights of Manhattan are so close, but this is our own world.

I stoop to pick up a leaf. The papery dryness has peeled away, and just the delicate veins of the skeleton remain.

"What's that?" Kal asks.

"I'm working on a new piece about the nature of decay," I reply. "This leaf was strong once, part of a bigger organism. It had a function, a goal. But the planet turned, and it's only now that the leaf is dead that its fragility is revealed."

I turn the leaf over and rest it on my palm. Kal picks it up.

"I wish I could see the world the way you do," he says, sounding almost sorrowful. "So much time wasted on the ugliness of life when I could have been appreciating the beauty and potential instead."

We reach a point where the path diverges, and I see lights through the brush. Kal pulls me along and into a clearing.

A tipi stands on its own raised decking. Tiny string bulbs light it, and a cooler sits off to one side. The tipi is open, strings holding the fabric back, and a lamp inside illuminates a bed covered in throws and pillows.

"Happy birthday, Dani."

I wheel around to look at Kal, my eyes brimming with happy tears.

"This is beautiful. But my father will kill you."

"Then I'd better say what I came here to say."

Kal leads me onto the decking. The lights are gorgeous, and the stars even more so. Despite the cold, I feel a deep, comforting warmth in my chest.

I'd have laughed in their face if someone had told me that this man would be the one I'd fall for.

On paper, he's everything I *don't* want.

An Antonov. A man from the Bratva life, where women are chattel. Something to tie me down, hold me back. Yet here we are.

Kal is speaking.

"I know you hate everything I stood for, Dani. For you, I turned my back on all of it. My siblings, my mother. My destiny, even."

What does he mean by that?

Kal closes his eyes for a moment, then opens them again, holding my gaze. In the low light, his pale blue irises almost glow.

"I'm throwing my lot in with you, *milaya*. Fuck knows what will come of it, but I don't care. I'm tired of the darkness." He rakes a hand through his hair and frowns as though he's struggling to find the right words. "All I know is you shine your light into me, and the bad thoughts scurry for cover like cockroaches."

I smile. This is breathtakingly romantic, despite the vermin-based analogy.

"I'm not a good man. I'm not even close. But you make me wanna be better, even if I have to tear myself to pieces and pull out all the rotten parts. It's gonna be agony, and I don't know what the fuck I'll have left over to work with. But Dani - I'm trying. I'm willing to claw my way out of the depths and let you warm me, let you bring me to fucking *life*."

Tears flow down my face. It's so hard to see Kal fight himself like this. It's as though he's never allowed himself to feel anything before. Now it's finally happening, it's hit him like a freight train.

He takes my hands in his.

"It could get ugly. This is all unchartered territory. You might not like what you find any more than I do. But I want to be a better man for you. If you'll have me."

I gawp stupidly as he sinks to one knee.

"I don't have a ring because I'm a moron and didn't plan this part." He smiles at my dumbstruck expression. "And because I think you might say no. It's a pain in the ass trying to convince the next woman to accept a second-hand diamond."

I give a half laugh, half sob, and pull my hand out of his so I can flip him off.

"That's my good girl," he says, and I flush with pleasure.

He's broken. He's a fucking mess. But he's a beautiful, fierce warrior, and like it or not, my heart is lost to him.

Kal looks up at me.

"Will you do me the honor of becoming my wife?" he asks.

I hurl myself to my knees, flinging my arms around his neck.

"I thought you were just playing with me," I whisper, raining kisses onto his lips. "I never thought you'd do this in a million years."

Kal wraps his arms around me, kissing me long and deep. I melt into his chest as he weaves his fingers through my hair.

"If that's not a yes," he murmurs against my mouth, "then this is about to be extremely embarrassing."

"Of course it's a yes!"

Kal stands up and pulls me to my feet. He opens the cooler and pulls out a bottle of champagne and two glasses. He hands the glasses to me.

"I thought you didn't like champagne," I say. "You said it was fucking disgusting."

"On the plane?" He unwraps the foil seal and grips the cork tightly, twisting the bottle. I'm reminded of something, and the image distracts me for a second before the cork flies off into the night, the fizz bubbling onto the ground. "I don't like it. But you do, and that's all that matters."

I giggle at his earnestness. "Sorry, but I lied. I was just trying to show some appreciation and be polite. I can't stand champagne either."

Kal rolls his eyes. "I've never done something like this before. I guess that's obvious. Never even been camping."

"This is hardly camping." I look around. "Oh, wait. No bathroom?"

"There's a chemical toilet thing just over there," Kal says, pointing, "and that's it. The romance has peaked."

I laugh as I put the glasses back in the cooler.

The bed feels good, and I lie down, patting the space beside me. Kal stretches out, kicking off his boots.

"I went camping with my father all the time when I was a kid," I say. "You never did things like that?"

"No. Erik wasn't the type. His mind was always on serious matters. That's the way of all strong men." He reaches out and tucks a loose lock of hair behind my ear.

I shake my head. "That's bullshit. My father is a strong man, but he's also the guy who always makes faces with my food, even now." I smile as I think of my Papa. "He's never tried to force me down any path. He's protective, and he always reminds me that I need to take more care, but he knows who I am."

Kal rests a hand on my hip, but he seems miles away. When he speaks, his voice is leaden.

"My stepfather didn't *know* me, and my mother doesn't care. She wanted me to be the image of Erik, and it's only recently that I started to see a different path."

"Is that why you came to us? To *me*?"

Kal looks furious, but his expression softens in an instant. He pulls me towards him, his lips firm and insistent on mine.

"You're my future," he murmurs between kisses, "and I will do whatever it takes to be worthy of a woman like you."

17

DANI

Kal's tongue delves into my mouth, and I welcome it, eager to taste him.

Everything I want is within reach.

Just like that, the threat to my family is over. Without her champion, Idina has no one to take us on, and the Pushkin Bratva can look toward a peaceful future.

Dreams I never dared to cling to are coming true. Kal Antonov wants me, for real. For *keeps*. I will have the love I want and the darkness I crave in the same glorious package.

And my father will have what he wants most. A happy daughter who, against all the odds, happens to be married to a Bratva man.

Kal's hand on the back of my neck disrupts my thoughts. He's feeling for my zipper.

"You are not allowed to wear this fucking thing ever again," he says. "What idiot designed this? There's no way into it!"

I laugh, pushing his jacket off his shoulders. I touch his chest as I unbutton his shirt, his skin warm under my hands.

With a grunt of frustration, Kal finally finds the zipper and glides it down, his hands hot and firm on my back.

"Are you cold?"

"A little," I say. He pulls a large woolen throw over us both.

"Better?"

I nod as he peels the jumpsuit away from my body. "But now I'm only wearing a thong. It would be best if you got naked too. Only fair."

Kal doesn't need any encouragement, and his clothes are on the floor in a matter of seconds. He rolls me onto my back and runs his tongue between my tits.

"These are mine," he says, "and I'm gonna remind you regularly by coming on them."

"I don't doubt it," I whisper.

My nipples are already hard from the cold air. Kal flicks them with his tongue, warming them with his lips until they are hot and firmer than ever. It's like my brain has short-circuited, and every lick pulls at my clit, making it swell.

"I'm in no hurry," Kal says, his hand sliding along my side and settling on my mound. "I'm gonna tease you a while."

"You know what?" I ask, sighing as he runs his fingertips over my pussy. "This isn't how it's done. Aren't Bratva marriages supposed to be for mercenary reasons, like to pay a debt or cement an alliance or something? This all seems so..." my voice trails away as Kal presses harder, "... civilized."

Kal kisses his way along my belly until his head rests against my inner thigh. He pulls my thong aside and inhales deeply, breathing in the scent of my arousal, and gives a low growl. His eyes meet mine.

"You think I'm fucking *civilized*?"

Without warning, he plunges two fingers deep into my pussy. I arch my back and gasp. He scissors his fingers inside me, stretching my sensitive inner walls as waves of sensation smash through me.

"Make no mistake, Dani. You light me up. But shadows are always darkest on the brightest days, and I'm no different. I brought out the nasty in you, but know this." He lashes at my clit with his tongue, and I cry out. "I'll honor and love you in the light, but when the darkness takes over, you're mine to ruin. I own you, right down to your bone marrow. All I want is to worship your body until you're sore and numb, yet still wanting more. Anything less than total submission isn't gonna fucking cut it. Understood?"

I gasp my assent as his tongue works my clit again.

His words are terrifyingly arousing. The intensity of his desire is beyond my experience, and I'm damn sure he means every word he says.

I will be married to a man who will put his depravity to work, servicing my pleasure as long as I play his filthy games.

Hot fucking damn.

Who do I thank for this? What did I do to deserve him?

Kal turns his hand around, curling his fingers slightly as he moves them. I yelp as they push against my most sensitive spot.

"Oh, *there* it is," he says, massaging me firmly as he sucks my clit. "No wonder you make such a mess when you come, you dirty girl."

Everything he says gives my nerves a renewed flash of pleasure, as though he's touching me everywhere at once. I can't decide whether I want him to shut the fuck up or keep whispering filthy sweetness to me until I climax from that alone.

Kal removes his fingers from inside me and sits up, taking the blanket with him. I didn't realize how hot I was, and the rush of cool air on my skin feels incredible.

He's a hell of a sight to behold. Broad-chested and muscled, his waist tapering into lean hips, his cock wet and swollen.

I want him inside me. The ache deep within is crippling.

"Turn over and get on all fours," he says. "I wanna hit that sweet spot hard, *milaya*, and get you coming all over me."

I turn around, my face in the pillow and my ass high.

Kal reaches under his pillow, his cock nudging my pussy as he leans around me.

He's holding something in front of my face. It's a whip with lots of strands and a handle, but I don't know what it's called.

Kal's chin grazes my shoulder.

"You want this?" he asks.

I nod.

"Good." He piles a couple of pillows in front of me. "Rest your chest on these. I want your hands holding your ass open."

I move, parting my cheeks to expose my smallest hole. I feel humiliated yet profoundly turned on, knowing I'm giving him what he wants.

Kal trails the whip down my back, dragging the tails over my tight pucker. He flicks it at my pussy, catching my clit slightly, and I jump.

I feel the hot, smooth head of his cock pushing between my pussy lips, and I groan with relief as he sinks his length into me. His hand slides up my spine and into my hair, grabbing a handful.

"Don't you let go of that ass, Dani," he says, pulling back from me. "Not for anything. If you do, I'll stop."

My pussy clutches his cock as he plunges back inside me. At that exact moment, Kal brings the whip down on my exposed asshole.

My body is confused, pain gouging through my pleasure. My clit throbs, my pussy juice running down my legs even as my ass stings and spasms. The sensations are all mixed up, and somehow it feels fantastic.

Kal pushes all the way into me so he can reach around and hold the whip to my face. With a flick of his wrist, he spins it around so the handle faces me.

"Get this good and wet," he says, bumping his hips against me, "because this is going in your asshole."

I part my lips, taking the whip handle into my throat. It's smooth and more petite than Kal's cock, but I want it well-lubricated. I let him push it deep enough to make me gag and bring up the thicker spit he needs.

"That's my good little slut," he murmurs. He pulls the whip out of my mouth and rests it against my asshole. "You keep holding yourself open. I can't wait to see you take this."

I bury my face in the pillow and try to relax as Kal works the end of the handle into me. It's tight, but his cock inside my pussy distracts me and helps me to loosen up. After a minute of tiny movements, the tip is lodged inside my ass.

Kal spits on me, and I feel the sudden wet warmth as his saliva runs over my skin.

"Breathe out on three. It's going in. One, two, three…."

He pushes the handle into my ass, and I scream. The searing pain gives way to an all-encompassing feeling of fullness as Kal lets go of my hair and grips my hips, pounding my pussy harder.

"Well done, *milaya*. Let go now and touch your clit while I fuck you."

I brace one arm beneath me and reach for my pussy with my free hand, rubbing my swollen clit rhythmically. My holes are stretched to the limit, the whip strands hanging from me like a tail. Kal gathers the loose tendrils in his hand, using them to move the whip handle around inside me.

It's more than I can take. My orgasm hits me so hard that I see stars, and a strangled scream of pleasure rings from my throat, my thighs shaking. My juice runs freely, soaking the bed beneath my knees.

Kal feels me convulse and slams his hips, pumping me full of his come. He holds me still as he twitches, ensuring I take all of it.

We don't move for a long time. Eventually, Kal takes hold of the still-wedged whip and strokes my shoulder gently with his other hand.

"Just relax your muscles," he says. With a firm pull, the whip is gone, leaving only a dull throb.

As we lie there, I begin to feel a chill. Kal notices me shivering and pulls the blankets over me once more.

"I don't have any clothes," I say, snuggling up to his warmth.

Kal sounds tired. "You think I'd remember a cat-o'-nine-tails but not bring you anything to wear? There's a suitcase under the bed with some things for you."

"And you managed it yourself? No concierge to help this time?"

He swats my ass. "I did it all. Are you okay? I know that was kinda intense."

"It was, but I'm fine. Will it always be like that for us?"

"No. I wanted to do the romantic thing and stare into your eyes, all that shit. But I stashed the whip in case the freak showed up to play, and whaddayaknow…"

I yawn. "What about my father?"

"He knew."

"About the whip?"

"Jesus, Dani." Kal laughs, pulling my head onto his chest. "About the proposal. He said he wants you to be happy, and if you accept, that's good enough for him. You and I can move into your place until we get somewhere of our own."

"So it's really over?" I mumble. "You're not my enemy anymore? We're safe?"

Sleep is overtaking me fast. If he replies, I don't hear it.

18

KAL

Dani's place is as sunny and bright as she is. We've been here a week, and already it's beginning to feel like home.

The loft space above the apartment serves as Dani's studio. She's there now, working on her paintings.

I need to go and talk to my mother.

I haven't seen Simeon since the Samhain Ball, and as much as that suits me, it's not a good sign. Idina and I have exchanged a couple of terse text messages, but she's gonna realize pretty soon that I'm not at the Pushkin home, ready to cut Fyodor down.

I'm going to marry Danica Pushkin. That makes me the heir to the Pushkin Bratva, legitimately and without force or skulduggery. Surely that will be enough for my mother? Her boy back in the fold, her family reconciled? I *want* to believe it, but I'm putting off the conversation. It's as though the lies and anger in my past might stain the present like spilled ink, and I want to block it all out.

Pippa bustles in through the front door, carrying a cardboard cup holder.

"Three large lattes," she says, "and one huge headache. It's crazy busy out there!"

"Christmas shopping," I say, taking the coffee cups and setting them on the kitchen counter. "Starts earlier every year."

"Aw, I love Christmas," Pippa trills.

I smile. Her posh English accent is fun to listen to.

"What do *you* like to do at Christmas, Kal?" Pippa asks, removing her scarf.

"Never been a big deal for my family."

December twenty-fifth has always been a significant day, but not because of Christmas.

Every year, Idina became more unpredictable as the holiday drew nearer. Picking fights with Erik, and after he died, picking fights with her kids, me especially. The rest of the time, she coddled and suffocated me with her attention, but on that particular holiday morning, she would get up early so she'd be good and drunk by the time I got out of bed. Then she ordered me to sit on the floor, and she would recline in her chair and stare at me, her eyes black as coal.

"Bastard," she would mutter. "You're disgusting. Blackhearted. Foul. Depraved."

I would sit on the floor and try not to listen. There would be no toys, just a stream of cruel words that I didn't understand.

One year, she went off crazier than ever.

"On Christmas morning when I was thirteen, my mother took my stepfather's gun. She sat in the car with the doors locked, the pistol in her mouth, as we kids cried and banged on the windows, begging her to stop."

"Holy shit." Pippa is frozen to the spot, hanging on my every word.

I didn't realize I was saying it aloud.

"I'm such a fuck-up," I say, leaning against the counter and rubbing my face with my palm. "I'm trying hard to pull away from it, but things are coming back to me all the time. Things I haven't thought about in years."

"You need to force yourself to let the light in, Kal. Even if it's blinding at first, you'll adjust." Pippa hands me two coffee cups. "Go see Dani. Talk to her."

I take the drinks and climb the stairs into the loft.

Dani's canvas is six feet square, propped on a stand. She has her back to me, her tongue at the corner of her mouth as she moves her brush through the paint.

"Are you feeling better?" I ask. "Pippa brought coffee. I didn't tell her you might be too sick to drink it."

Dani turns and smiles at me. She looks pale, and I frown. I put the cups on the floor and go to her, pressing my hand to her forehead.

"You're not feverish, but you look like hell. How many times have you thrown up?"

"Twice. It's alright, Kal. I'll be okay. But you're gonna have to chill out a bit."

"Why do I have to do that? I'm worried about you. There's no fucking air in here." I pick up her paint can, sniffing it. "And what's *in* this shit, anyway?"

"It's water-based. And it's not as though I'm drinking it," she laughs. "I don't want the coffee either. Not a good idea in my condition."

What?

"Wait a minute," I say, grabbing her hand. "You're…?"

"Yep," she grins. "At least a couple of months. I did a test yesterday and another this morning to be sure."

My heart is pounding. She's caught me totally off guard, and I don't know how to feel.

I'm gonna be a father. Me. The most dysfunctional asshole ever.

"I don't know how to be a parent," I say. The words come out of me without a thought to how it sounds. "I've never known a happy family. What if I fuck it up?"

Dani turns my hand over in hers and brings it to her face, resting it on her cheek.

"*We're* a family now," she says. "You and me and the baby. We've brought a poisonous vendetta to a peaceful conclusion, and now it's about the future." She kisses my thumb. "I promised I'd help you heal, Kal. I believe in you."

I take her waist in my hands and pull her body to me. She wraps her arms around my neck.

"What do you need?" I ask. "Tell me how I can help. Nothing is too much to ask."

Dani laughs. "I don't need you to walk over water for me, but if you could go get me some peppermint tea, I'd be grateful."

Peppermint tea. Something Dani and Idina both like.

They could have gotten along in another life, but I don't think it's gonna happen.

When Vera showed signs of spirit, my mother soon stomped that out. Dani would get the same treatment.

∼

I'm still thinking about my sister when I see her on the corner of the street. It's as though my thoughts summoned her.

She's standing there as though she's waiting for someone. It can only be me, but seeing as I wasn't expecting her, I figure she's been there a while.

"S'up, bro," she says as I reach her. "How's domestic bliss?"

"So I guess word travels fast," I say.

"It can travel a lot fucking faster. But the headline is that you sold us out for pussy, and I thought I'd come and see for myself." She smirks. "Luckily for you, Idina doesn't know yet. What's it worth to me to keep my mouth shut?"

"You don't know what's happening, so what are you even gonna say? Plans have changed. I'll tell her the whole story when I'm ready."

Vera lights a cigarette, blowing smoke into my face. "You'll destroy her, Kal. All that time and energy wasted on you. Years and years. She drilled it into you - you have a job to do. You have to avenge our father—"

"Erik was not my father," I say, "and I'm glad. The cunt did some terrible things, Vera. Don't you remember what he was like? Why did we let Idina peddle these lies about him being a great man? He was a piece of shit."

Vera slaps me across the face.

I'll let her have that one. After all, I'm talking about her father, and a few weeks ago, I'd have fucked up anyone who said what I said just now.

"Idina is a difficult person, Kal, but she's all I have. I can't allow myself to think too badly of her, or I'll have to face up to things I can't fucking cope with. What then?"

She sounds tired and somehow younger, her tone lacking its usual bite. I'm overwhelmed by sadness.

I wish so much that Vera and I were different people. Better people. But we're not. If I tried to hug her now, she'd think I was attacking her and claw my eyes out.

"Go away, Vera," I say. "Tell Idina whatever you like, but the Pushkin Bratva will be mine. It's just gonna take a little longer. But we don't have to risk my and everyone else's lives to recover what we lost."

"Whatever you say." Vera drops her cigarette, grinding it with her heel. "But Idina's got Simeon in her ear, looking for his chance to shine. You better get your fucking act together before that pretty little whore of yours ends up dead."

I walk away towards the 7-Eleven. As I enter the store, I look over my shoulder. My sister crosses the road, heading around the corner and out of sight.

～

I find the tea easily. I pick up some gingerbread cookies and Gatorade, staring into space as the shop girl rings it up.

I have to tell Dani and her family the truth.

The danger is still there, and it's because of me.

All my lies became truths as time went on, but the way it began was ugly and sick. How can I live with myself if I don't come clean and beg forgiveness?

Idina deserves the truth, too. She's getting at least some of what she wanted. And she does love me in her way. She will understand, and if she can see what I see, she may learn and heal too.

I've never had anything to hope for before now. But my new family is the route to my redemption.

～

"Why didn't she fucking wait for me? I would have gone with her."

Pippa looks at me like I've grown another head.

"What the fuck is the matter with you? She went to get more paint from the art supply place. And besides," Pippa sneers at me, "she doesn't answer to *you*. You're her fiancé, not her jailer."

"I'm also supposed to be keeping her safe."

"From what?" Pippa says, gesturing around the room. "Dust bunnies? I thought all your stupid mafia feuding was over now."

"You have no idea what you're talking about," I snarl. I throw the groceries onto the floor, running back outside.

She's gonna be okay. Just call her.

I call Dani The line rings and rings, but she doesn't pick up.

When I try a second time, it goes straight to voicemail. I wait for the beep.

"Dani," I say, walking fast along the sidewalk, "where the fuck are you? You can't just do whatever you want. Call me back *now*."

I'm getting into the car as my phone vibrates in my pocket. I snatch it out, answering it as I slam the car door.

"Simeon! Where the fuck is she?"

I can hear the mirth in my brother's voice. "So it's true. You sold us out for that Pushkin slut. If you had to betray your own family, couldn't you have done it without your cock hanging out?"

"If you hurt her, I'll kill you."

"Oh, like you did to poor old Vito Serra?" Simeon says. "The dirty bastard just wanted to fuck your precious girl's whore mouth. Is that such a crime? But you had to kill him by throwing him off a fucking balcony. It's a miracle no one else was injured."

So that's who it was. No great loss. A Sicilian mafia elder known for being a rapist and an all-around scumbag. Presumably, he was scraped off the sidewalk without much fuss, and that was that.

"I will rip your tongue out for talking that way about my fiancée, Simeon. Where is she? I swear I'll…"

I look up to see Dani walking around the corner, and I hang up.

19

DANI

The last few weeks have been a whirlwind, but it feels right.

Kal was a feared and hated enemy, yet now he's a new member of my family. It happened naturally and seamlessly, with no drama, and I can't believe my luck. My husband-to-be is Bratva, but he's also utterly devoted to me, and we're marrying for love. Unheard of in our world.

I didn't realize my pill had failed. It stops my periods completely, so I never thought about it until a few days ago when I started with the nausea. It was Pip who urged me to take a test, and there it was, plain as day. Two little blue lines that meant my life was about to change yet again.

If only I could nix this rolling sickness in my belly. I belch and wince as I turn onto my street.

Kal is right there, getting out of his car. He looks furious.

"Hey," I say. "You okay? Did something happen?"

"What the *fuck*, Dani?" Kal asks. He bangs his fist on the hood of the car, and I jump. "You can't just do whatever you want. Pippa said you went to the art shop, so I called. You didn't fucking pick up."

I dump my bag on the ground.

This is what I was afraid of. The controlling bullshit is starting already.

"I was busy buying paint, genius!" I tap my temple with my fingertip. "Think about it, Kal. I'm an artist. I'm working hard to rebuild my collection so I can have a comeback exhibition and get on with the life I had *before I fucking met you*. So funnily enough, I didn't make answering your call a priority!"

Kal frowns. "The exhibition is gonna have to be put on hold. I'm not happy about you putting yourself out there again after what happened last time."

"You mean when all my art, my work that meant so much to me, went up in fucking flames?" I laugh. "And at what arbitrary point in the future will you, oh Master, decide it is safe?"

"That's not the fucking point!"

I raise my hand above my eyes and squint, looking past Kal and all around. He throws his hands in the air in exasperation.

"What are you looking for?" he says.

"I'm searching for a fuck to give."

I turn away and walk into the house, Kal hot on my heels. Pippa is in the lounge, but when she sees the look on my face, she scurries away to her bedroom, closing the door behind her.

"You don't understand," Kal is saying. "I have concerns about your safety."

"Like what?"

Kal looks at his feet for a second before meeting my eyes. "Just thoughts. You're a Bratva princess and my fiancée. You're pregnant. I don't want anything to happen to you."

He didn't say 'anything bad.' He said 'anything,' and there's a fucking difference.

"So that's it? I *was* me, Danica Pushkin, but now I'm just Mrs. Antonov, mother to your baby and your personal fucktoy? Because you'd better believe me when I say I'm not falling for this."

Kal's face closes down, his features freezing as though he's turning into a waxwork before my eyes. He stares at me impassively as he speaks.

"I have no time to sit around here arguing. You will be safe at your parent's house. I have things to do."

I try to ignore the sting as my eyes fill with tears.

I won't let him make me cry. He pulled me off my pedestal and dashed me to the ground, just like I feared he would. Men like him don't know any other way to be. But he coaxed me with pretty lies and blistering passion, making me believe there could be a way for us to be happy together. Knowing I'm too far gone to let go of that belief.

I hate myself for letting my guard down. Even now, his expression is softening, and I'm willing him to say something that will make it all okay.

"Dani, look. I'm sorry, alright?"

Kal reaches for me, and I try to turn away, but I can't. His hand caresses the back of my neck.

"You know I'm broken. But you promised me you'd be there for the ugly stuff and right now, I need some grace. Will you give me just a little?"

I know I shouldn't let him get around me. He lost his shit with me for leaving my house to get paint. What else is he gonna get angry about?

I push my doubts down for now. It's one incident. We won't get through our lives without arguments.

"I left my paint outside," I say. "I'll bring it in and change into something more comfortable. Then fine, if you say so. I'll go."

Kal kisses my forehead. "Good girl. You can take your peppermint tea with you."

"This is how it goes, sis. They start off saying all the right things, then boom. You get married, and they decide you're just another thing they own."

I knew what Mel would say about it. But I can't bring myself to tell her or my parents about the baby.

It doesn't matter now whether I marry Kal. I'm bound to him for life no matter what.

Mel hands me my teacup. "I swear, if I'd have been the one who got murdered, my husband would have tried to claim me on the homeowner's insurance. When I voiced an independent thought, he acted as though I was malfunctioning. You know how people hit their appliances when they stop working properly?"

I breathe deeply. The steam from the tea is comforting, and the peppermint scent is helping my stomach to settle.

"I know," I say, taking a sip. "But it's not as though I didn't try. I didn't *want* to fall for him, but now it's too late. I love every possessive, arrogant bone in his body, and I would rather be under his control than without him. That's sick, isn't it?"

"It's love," Mel says, "or a *kind* of love, at least. It's not healthy, but so much of what makes life worth living is objectively bad for you. Should people drink alcohol, do drugs, eat fudge cake, smoke, or do disgusting, depraved things in bed? Probably not. But isn't that the point of those things? That they're wrong?"

She's right, of course. For me, Kal is like heroin. Once I let him under my skin, I could never get enough, and I'll destroy myself just to keep getting that fix.

I have said nothing about the exhibition, either.

Kal knows what it means to me. He was there when the gallery burned down. He saw everything I worked for reduced to ashes. Now he wants me to abandon it after I worked so hard to build it up again?

I bared more than my body to him. I let him see my hopes, my fears, and my dreams. He knows I want my freedom.

And yet, here I am, sitting around and waiting for him to come and tell me I can carry on with my life.

Kal Antonov has no right to do this to me. No one does.

A wave of sickness bubbles up from my stomach, and I groan. Mel helps me into the house and settles me on the couch in the lounge.

My Mama is sitting in the armchair, nursing a small glass of white wine. She nods at the bottle on the table.

"Kill or cure," she says. "Worth a try?"

I grimace at the thought. "No, I can't. I mean, I don't think it's a good idea."

Mel leaves the room, and Mama sits forward, her elbows on her knees. She steeples her fingers under her chin.

"How far along are you, Dani?"

I close my eyes, pretending I didn't hear her.

Shit. How can she *tell*?

"There's no use in trying to hide it," Mama says. "You look just like I did when I was having you. And it's the only time I ever wanted that godforsaken mint tea."

I open my eyes and smile. "You got me. I don't know exactly how far, just a couple of months."

"Have you told Kal? Is that why he dropped you off without a word and disappeared?"

"He knows. He just wants me to be safe."

I don't know why I'm defending him, but Mama sees the doubt in my eyes.

"You know something, Dani? Whatever you believe, you're right."

"What does that mean?"

"You believe Kal is a good guy who loves you enough to forsake his family? Then he is. If you think he's just another Bratva asshole who only wants a woman to control, you'll soon be proved right on that too. You know why?"

I shake my head.

"Because people see whatever their prejudice and fear show them. We filter out all the information that doesn't fit our bias because it's so incredibly hard to be wrong about something, especially our principles."

Mama takes a swig of her wine and tops it up from the bottle.

"On the night of your birthday, while you were out with Kal, your Papa went to meet a rival from out of town. There were rumors he was going to push into our territory and cause problems, but your father went to that meeting believing that he need only assert his position reasonably, and all would be well. He didn't find out until later that the rival had a pistol under the table the whole time, pointing at him."

My eyes widen. "They could have killed him. Isn't this why he rarely gets his hands dirty?"

"Dani, you're missing the point," Mama says. "Papa is still here because he showed good faith. The other guy came to him with paranoia and hostility, but in the face of your father's decency and goodwill, it all went away. They negotiated a deal, and now the rival is actually working for us."

My tea is lukewarm now. I put the cup on the table.

"Please put me out of my misery, Mama. What are you getting at?"

Mama smiles. "Dani, you're in love. It's obvious. You don't have to have your pistol pointed at him the whole time, ready to blow him away if he slips up. He's only human. If your father can see the good in Kal Antonov, surely you can?"

I open my mouth to speak, but she shows me her palm. The conversation is over.

"Think on it a while."

She stands, heading out of the room.

"Mama?" I say.

"Yes, my Dani?"

"Please don't tell Papa about... you know."

"I won't. Now try to rest."

20

KAL

Strange how much difference a change of perspective can make.

My mother has a house, but it's not a *home*. I never realized before how impersonal the place is.

No pictures on the walls, not even of Erik. No photo albums, no keepsakes. No ornaments or books, or flowers. Nothing suggests that the person here has a family or even a personality.

But that's not the case. It's just that Idina's personality is deeply disordered, and it hurts me profoundly to know it.

I thought we were normal.

I believed Idina's mercurial nature, smothering one minute and cold and distant the next, was to be expected in a mother. I thought Erik's brutalizing of Simeon and favoritism of me was character-building, meant to make me strong.

And I thought women were to be used and discarded. I didn't know I'd meet one like *her*.

Dani Pushkin turned my world upside down and shook it fucking hard.

I was a man of purpose, ready to fulfill my destiny and forge a new empire in blood and suffering. She and her family told me some hard truths, and I had to acknowledge the bullshit I'd been force-fed for so long. They could have cast me out, but they gave me a chance I didn't even fucking deserve.

And that's why I'm here.

My siblings know about Dani. Just today, Vera said Simeon is trying to step into my shoes, and that's a dangerous prospect because he hates me more than he loves our mother. Dani is his likely target unless I can get Idina to muzzle the fucker and get him back on his leash.

My mother appears in the doorway. She's been crying, and her eyes look sore.

"You betrayed me, Kal. I never thought you could be so cruel."

There was a time I'd have been drowning in guilt to hear her say that. Now it sounds hollow. She's not capable of that depth of feeling.

My turn to be the manipulative one.

"What do you mean?" I ask. "We've achieved a stunning victory."

Idina narrows her eyes, her lips a thin line. I sit down, but she doesn't move.

"You aren't looking at this logically, Idina. I marry the Pushkin girl and become the only man other than Fyodor in the immediate family. That gives me an automatic claim, but without any of the bloodshed. I don't have to risk my life, and there's no chance of a repeat of what happened to Erik."

Idina's eyes bore into me, her voice colder than liquid nitrogen.

"That isn't good enough. I want Fyodor dead. I want all of them fucking *dead*."

The little kid in me is still so afraid of her, but I'm not backing down. My world is bigger now.

"I won't do it. Do you understand?"

Idina tries to speak, but I cut her off. "No. Shut the fuck up. I'm sick of being lied to. I'm done. You have nothing to threaten me with."

"I have Simmi," she says. She has never called him a pet name in his life before now. "I can always depend on my Simeon."

I shake my head. "Look at yourself. What are you talking about? Simeon can't pick up where I left off. Without me, you can't have your glorious fucking coup, so why keep this up? You could just let it go."

Idina's smile is a rare sight and never was it less sincere than it is right now. Her lips stretch over her teeth, and I try to hide my disgust.

"We'll see," she says. "But you can't escape from fate, my son. And neither can little Danica Pushkin."

I can't kill my mother. No way.

Do I have any cards left to play?

"Dani is pregnant," I say. "From the dates, it must have happened the first time we were together. Where does fate fit into *that*?"

Idina closes her eyes. "Mark my words, Kal. I will have my revenge, with or without your help. Now get out."

I head for the door, my heart heavy.

I may never set foot in this house again. Despite everything, it stings.

Just like the Pushkin mansion, our house has ghosts, but the specters are the ones who are happy and free. Everywhere I look, I see shadows of the family we could have been, living their lives with love and togetherness.

Idina's voice pierces my sorrow.

"Kal?"

"What?" I say, turning around.

I'll take anything—any sign she understands.

"Congratulations. At least we know you have the balls for something. And leave your fucking key."

I toss it onto the hallway rug, and I'm gone.

~

"No fucking way. Are you *insane*?"

I pinch the bridge of my nose and blink, trying to stave off the headache that has been creeping in since I spoke to Vera.

"Dani, we have to get out of here," I say. "I don't know for sure, but I think my brother is gonna try and hurt you to get at me."

"Why would he do that? What's the problem? I thought you cut them all off."

What could I say to make the truth seem less fucked up?

So first, I fucked you because I wanted to. Then it was my idea to burn down the gallery with you inside, destroying your work and risking your life so I could rescue you and earn a chance to get close to Fyodor. I was gonna kill him and become Pakhan, only to change my mind because I was wrong about so much. Now I don't know what's gonna happen, but because you're everything to me, you're in danger.

It doesn't sound good, even in my head.

"I love you, Dani."

She draws a sharp breath before frowning at me.

"That's a low blow, Kal, to say it is when you're forcing me to abandon the people I love. No. We're staying."

I'm exasperated and proud at the same time. She's not taking any of my shit, and why should she? She's right. I'm asking her to do something extreme without giving her the necessary information.

"Dani, I'm being nice now. But I am prepared to piss you off a lot more than this if it means keeping you safe."

"You can't just move me from place to place!" she cries. "I am a person and don't belong to you."

"Yes, you fucking *do!*" I yell back. I know it's the wrong thing to say, but I'm not thinking straight.

I want to get her away from here. Or maybe I'm ruining her life. My mother doesn't believe I can be anything other than the black-hearted, vengeful puppet she raised. Who's to say she's wrong?

Marta and Mel look from me to Dani and back again. Fyodor stands up and takes me aside.

"There's something you're not telling us," he murmurs, "and we *are* going to talk about it. But not here."

I look over his shoulder at Dani. She's glaring at me.

Fyodor turns to his wife and daughters. I try to catch Dani's eye, but she won't look at me.

I have to come clean, or I'll lose her.

"Kal and I are gonna take a drive, maybe get a drink," Fyodor says. "I'll leave Brutus guarding the gate. You'll be fine."

Fyodor and I leave the lounge and walk outside. Brutus is waiting for us, and Fyodor gives him a nod.

Brutus frisks me, patting down my body and reaching inside my jacket.

"Buy me a drink first, big guy," I say.

Brutus ignores me and finishes his checks. "He's clean. No weapons."

We leave him at the gate and head for the garage.

"You're driving," Fyodor says, "but you'll go where *I* tell you."

∼

"Marta and the girls will be safe at home," Fyodor says, "but only because you're not there. I want to believe in you, Kal, for the sake of my Dani's poor heart, but you'd better be prepared to tell me the whole truth."

I nod.

My eyes dart around, trying to see everything at once, as though hypervigilance might be enough to stave off disaster. I need to stop the car. I can't sit in a bar or even drive around having this conversation. My nerves are fucking shot.

"There." Fyodor points. "Parking garage. Find a spot far from any other vehicles and park up."

It doesn't take a genius to figure out why this is his destination of choice. When Fyodor hears what I have to tell him, he might lose his shit and kill me there and then. The less chance there is of anyone seeing that, the better.

The third floor has no cars on it, and I pull up in a bay, shutting off the engine.

I lean against the seat and close my eyes.

"Remember when you told me my choices weren't easy?" I say.

"Yeah. I told you to be wise."

Fyodor unfastens his seatbelt and taps my shoulder, and I open my eyes, turning to him.

"Are you being wise, Kal? Or are you being fucking stupid?"

The figure outside the car moves so quickly that I think I'm imagining it. The glass in the passenger window shatters into thousands of tiny pebbles.

"What the fuck?" Fyodor yells.

I'm trying to undo my seatbelt, but I'm too slow.

A hand reaches through the empty window frame, holding a spanner.

With a dull thud, the attacker brings the weapon down onto Fyodor's skull. The bow isn't hard enough to knock him out, but he's definitely subdued, his head lolling against the door.

The figure sticks his head through the window. I know who it is before he pulls down the bandana covering his mouth.

"Good job, Kal," Simeon says. "I knew you'd come through for us."

Fyodor is trying to say something.

"Kal...ambush? You fucking..." His voice fades into semi-conscious mumbling.

Simeon is laughing. I swipe my fist at him, but he pulls away before the punch connects. As I scramble out of the driver's side, he turns to speak to someone behind him.

"You see? I told you I could do it!"

I look over the roof of the car, and there she is.

My mother.

21

DANI

"They've been gone a while."

Mama is uncharacteristically jittery. She's usually calm and collected, but now she's pacing the room, pausing every minute to look out the window.

Brutus stands guard by the gates at the end of our driveway, Kalashnikov in hand. I can't remember a time when he's ever felt the need to do that before.

Mel is watching Mama, her brow furrowed. I can tell she's worried too. It's maddening just sitting around and waiting for a resolution.

I can hear the grandfather clock in the hallway ticking away as it has always done. I used to love the sound, but right now, I want to take a sledgehammer to it because every second that passes is torture.

The two men I love most in the world are deciding my future. It's precisely what I've always tried to avoid - a total loss of my autonomy.

Either Kal will convince my father to let us leave, or my father will prevent it from happening, in which case Kal might abandon me. And I'm caught in the middle, a pawn in these fucking stupid games.

No matter what happens now, it won't be *my* choice.

My mother makes her thousandth window check and frowns.

"There's someone outside."

The question is out before I can stop myself.

"Is it Kal?"

"*Jesus*, Dani," Mel says. "I thought you were better than this. That guy wanted to take you away from us for no better reason than he thought you were in danger. He's the one who brought all this bullshit to our lives. And now you're pining for the bastard?" She slumps back into her chair. "We should *all* have known better. Fucking Antonovs!"

I ignore her and join Mama at the window.

It's a woman, maybe about the same age as me. She's shouting at Brutus through the gate, but I can't hear the words. The security light catches her movements and bathes her in cold white light.

She looks straight at me, and I know who she is. The eyes are unmistakable.

"That's Kal's sister," I say. "Vera."

Mel is on her feet. "Why would she be here?" she asks me.

"I don't know. I'm gonna talk to her."

"Your father has gone somewhere with Kal and hasn't returned, and you want us to let another Antonov into our home?" Mama says. "No. She's not coming in here."

I look again at Vera. She's wearing a sweater dress and long boots. Nowhere to hide a weapon. She's still mouthing off at Brutus.

I go to the front door and open it, my mother and sister behind me. Vera looks past Brutus, calling to me.

"Dani! I need to talk to you, bitch. Open the fucking gate."

"I'm gonna see what she wants," I say, taking my coat from the stand and putting it on. "She might know what's happening."

I walk down the path.

"Brutus, it's alright. Just let her in. Nothing's gonna happen."

He unlocks the gate. Vera pushes it open, nearly knocking him over. Brutus retreats and sits on the wall.

"Asshole," Vera sneers at him.

We're standing in the garden, a few feet of space between us. The air is so cold that I can see my breath.

"Is your father here?" she asks. "Where's Kal?"

"They're out," I say. "What do you want?"

"You're not gonna invite me in?" Vera puts a hand on her chest in mock outrage. "How fucking *rude*."

"I thought about it, but no. I don't think you're here to pay a friendly house call."

Vera looks around the garden, scowling. "It's pretty here,"

she says. "Can't wait to move in." Her eyes stop on the jasmine, and she looks like she might burst into tears.

"What are you talking about?" I ask.

"You are the stupidest, most naïve little slut on earth. Not only did you open your legs for my brother, but you thought he rescued you from a fire because he *happened* to be there, like a guardian angel? You deserve everything you're gonna get."

Mama can't hear from the doorway, but she can see my face.

"Dani, come inside," she calls. I ignore her.

"What are you trying to tell me, Vera?" I ask.

"We set you up, you moron. Right from the start, this has been one big joke to Kal. Simeon and I burned down the gallery, but it was your fiancé's idea."

My knees threaten to buckle. *No. She's lying, surely.*

Vera continues. "So Kal rescued you, and that softened up your Papa real quick. Manipulated his way into your home *and* your pussy, and now he's gonna be the next Pakhan, just like he planned."

I never thought about that before. Is that the real reason he asked me to marry him? To take control?

Of course. He's an *Antonov*.

Real life right there, kicking me when I'm down.

"You're just another Bratva whore, and that's all there is to it. Kal knows you won't fight him," Vera raises her voice, "because you're having his baby."

"Oh, sweet Jesus!" Mel cries. I can hear Mama trying to calm her as she breaks into sobs.

"So he's been in touch this whole time," I say.

"Yep. Fun and games all around."

Kal lied when he said he'd cut his family off.

He told his sister about our baby. Given that *I* only told him today, he shared the joyous news with her pretty fucking quickly.

"But he's been trying to get me to leave with him. Why would he—"

"Fuck knows. Maybe he just wanted to be sure his broodmare would be safe and far from here when he made his move. But you wouldn't fucking go, would you?" Vera raises her eyebrows at me. "The only person who could stop all this now is your beloved Papa. And where *exactly* is he, by the way?"

My blood chills.

"Tell me one thing," I say. "If what you're telling me is true, why didn't Kal just kill my father when he got the chance?"

Vera shrugs. "He's wanted nothing but vengeance on your family since he was a kid. Killing Fyodor is one thing, but breaking his daughter's heart once he got bored with fucking her? What a bonus!"

My father is in danger, and it's my fault. My carelessness and stupidity got us here.

Papa told me to keep away from the Antonovs. He warned me to be careful, to remember that I'm a Bratva princess and people might take advantage of me. But when Kal 'rescued' me, he used my father's honorable nature against him to infiltrate our family, and I was so distracted by my attraction to him I didn't see what was right in front of me.

Vera moves closer.

"Don't," I say. "Stay where you are. I don't want a fight."

I'm surprised to see her eyes shimmer with tears.

"Kal is just using you," she says quietly. "He told me so himself. There's no good in any of us Antonovs."

I see a thousand stories in her eyes.

It's the same wounded look Kal gets when his memories get on top of him. She's seen things she should never have witnessed and experienced things she'd do anything to forget.

"Why are you even here?" I ask.

"I never had what you have, Dani. I just wanted to see your perfect life shatter. "

It's true. The Antonovs *are* poison, and no matter how much I want to believe otherwise, maybe there's no cure.

Vera walks away from me, pulling the gate open. Brutus stands up, but I shake my head at him.

"Hey," I say. Vera turns to look at me. "What the fuck is wrong with you people? Why are you like this?"

"Because we can't choose our fate. Some things are meant to be, and no amount of love or hope or optimism will ever change it."

I want to throw down. If it wasn't for my delicate condition, I'd fucking punch her for saying those things.

But it's not necessary because it doesn't feel like Vera has won. She looks defeated, and somehow I think she's felt that way for a long time.

I say nothing more as she walks to her car, Brutus closing the gates behind her. She pulls away into the night, gone just as suddenly as she arrived.

When I go back inside, Mel is sitting on the floor in the hallway, still sobbing. Mama is beside her, holding her hand.

"Dani, you've ruined your life," Mel says through her tears. "What the fuck are we gonna do?"

"I don't know. Vera told me she and her brother started the gallery fire on Kal's orders."

Mama frowns. "Do you believe her?"

"She's got no reason to lie. You were wrong, Mama. I was wrong too. We saw good in Kal, but it was a front."

I sit on the floor beside my mother and sister.

"I told Fyodor to give the boy a chance," Mama whispers. "It's my fault that it's come to this."

"No, Mama," I say, resting my head on her shoulder. "It's mine."

There's nothing for us to do now but wait.

22

KAL

My mother is smiling. It might be the first genuine smile I've ever seen on her face. Even her eyes have a sparkle to them.

"Kal, I'm so glad you changed your mind!" she says, walking towards me. "I knew you wouldn't abandon me when I needed you most."

Simeon reaches into his jacket.

He has a gun. Who thought giving that twitchy fuck a firearm was a good idea? He'll sneeze and blow his own head off.

"I wanna shoot Fyodor," he says. "Let me do it, Mama."

The kid has fucking lost it.

Is Idina letting him call her Mama? What next? Is she gonna be breastfeeding him?

"Leave him," Idina says. "He's not going anywhere."

Depraved Royals

Simeon sighs and points the gun at me instead.

"You didn't have to make it this complicated, Kal," Idina says. "You don't want to kill Fyodor. That's alright. You brought him here for us so that Simeon can do it. But we still need you to take control of the Pushkin Bratva."

Simeon looks from me to her. "Mama, you said you wanted me to kill Fyodor. You never said Kal was still going to be Pakhan!"

"Don't be ridiculous, Simeon," Idina spits. "Of *course* I told you that. This is exactly why I can't depend on you. Either you don't listen in the first place, or you don't fucking remember."

I watch Simeon's face contort with confusion. Two decades of gaslighting have left him with barely any sense of reality apart from hers. I was much the same until I got away from her mind games.

"I don't want this," I say. "I won't play along, not on your terms. You were wrong about everything."

"Everything I did was for *you*," Idina hisses. "Now we can take what should be ours. All we have to do is kill Fyodor, and that's it. You'll have achieved your destiny and avenged your father, just like you always wanted."

"No!" I cry. "It's what *you* always wanted, and you never gave me a choice to refuse. I don't have to be like Erik."

"You *are* like Erik. You are a loveless, cold-hearted man, and nothing will change that. Even if you ran away to live with the girl and raise a family, you'd end up hurting her. You're probably doing it already."

I think of the last time I saw Dani's face. Full of mistrust. She lived her life happily and without fear before I came around and fucked her up.

I've been worrying about her safety, ready to raise hell if she came to harm. But in the end, it'll be *me* who hurt her the most, no matter how hard I tried to be better.

Idina's right. I can't escape it. The darkness is who I am.

The car's engine starts, and we all turn to look. Simeon whips his arm around and points the gun at the back windshield.

Fuck me.

Fyodor is not only alive. He's conscious and in the driver's seat, revving the engine like crazy. He releases the parking brake, and the car shoots toward us.

"You fucking traitorous cunt, Kal!" Fyodor screams over the squeal of the tires. "How could you do this to her?"

Simeon fires, the bullet ricocheting harmlessly off a pillar. I'm vaguely aware of Idina screaming as I rush at him, knocking the gun from his hand as we both fall to the ground.

I have to move, or Fyodor will run me over. Only moments to act.

Live or die.

I grab Simeon by the shoulders and roll, dragging him out of the way. The car's tires miss my head by an inch.

Fyodor screeches to a halt, the car now facing forwards. He revs the engine again.

I can't keep hold of Simeon. He's on his feet again, swooping down to pick up the gun. I think he's going to shoot me for a moment, but he's advancing on the car, laughing maniacally.

"For you, Mama!" he cries. "Watch this!"

He raises his hand and fires, the bullet punching a hole through the windshield. Fyodor's shoulder jolts, blood spattering on the seat.

Simeon turns to face our mother, waving the gun triumphantly.

"I did it! Were you watching?"

Holy shit. Simeon killed him?

No. The old man is made of sterner stuff than that.

With a blood-curdling roar, Fyodor floors it. Simeon doesn't turn around quick enough to react.

The car smashes into him, snapping his legs like twigs. His body flies over the roof and smacks into the concrete, landing in a crumpled heap.

Idina gives a long, piercing scream.

Fyodor slams on the brakes so he doesn't hit the wall and then turns to drive down the ramp and out. He doesn't look back.

It all happened so fast.

I'm frozen to the spot, my chest burning. I realize I haven't taken a breath in ages. As I fill my lungs, trying to get a grip, my mother flings herself onto Simeon's broken body. She's sobbing, pulling at his shirt.

"My Simeon," she wails. She looks up, jabbing her finger at me. "You killed your brother! How could you do this to me?"

As I watch, appalled, she composes herself. She sits up and wipes her eyes, and just like that, the show of emotion is over, locked away inside.

"It's okay, Kal. You can make it up to me." She holds out a hand, but I don't move. "Come, my son. Fyodor is weak. We can finish him off, and everything will be as it should be. That bastard killed your brother *and* your father!"

I stare at her. Her eyes are wild, desperate.

"First it was me who killed Simeon, then Fyodor. But you're full of shit. *You* killed Simeon, but not today. You snuffed him out years ago with your abuse, leaving only an empty shell of a man."

I walk to where the gun lies on the ground and pick it up. Idina never takes her eyes off me for a second.

"I won't hurt you," I say, "but I won't help you, either. You lied to me every day for my entire life. Nothing we ever had was real. I thought you loved me, but you only know how to use people. I know what love is, and now thanks to you, I may have lost it forever."

"You think I don't know love?" Idina cocks her head at me. "There was a man once, Kal. I'd have done anything for him, but everyone warned me away - they said he was a bad guy. I wanted to believe there was good in him.

"On Christmas day, I told my parents I would stay with a friend, but I went to him instead and told him I loved him. I was just seventeen, and he was forty. He told me he loved me too and wanted to have sex with me."

Depraved Royals

Is this bullshit? It could be. But she's talking weirdly, almost like I'm not here.

"I said I wasn't ready and wanted to announce our engagement first, but he didn't like that. We argued. He beat me and then held me prisoner for two days, forcing himself on me many times. He only let me go because he knew I loved him still and wouldn't tell anyone what he'd done."

I feel like I'm gonna throw up.

"That's who your father really was, Kal," Idina says. "Erik knew. He chose you to mold in his image because he knew you came from real evil and would never be able to escape that."

I back away towards the door that leads to the stairwell.

"Do you still think you can be a good man? Your blood is tainted with depravity. You're sick to the core."

Gotta get away from her. I can't listen to her twisted words anymore.

She's shouting now, still sitting beside Simeon's corpse.

"You'll ruin that girl's life. She deserves better than a bastard like you. Vera told her everything you did, and she'll never let you near that baby in a million fucking years." She's laughing. "Go! At least I know the Pushkins are gonna suffer for a long time, thanks to you!"

I'm everything I feared I was. I bring pain and death wherever I go. Love is too beautiful and tender for someone as impure and sullied as me, and now I know the badness truly does run deep.

I think of some of the things I've done to Dani. Am I sick? Have I corrupted her? Maybe I just imagined she was into it to justify taking what I wanted.

I run down the stairs to the ground level and find the attendant dead in his booth. Figures. Even Simeon could handle one overweight security guy.

Idina's car is parked on the first floor. I know they must have followed me here, but I don't know how I didn't see them.

I return to the security booth and rummage under the counter until I find a crowbar. The driver's door is easy enough to jimmy open, and as I climb into my mother's car, a memory comes flooding back. I wonder if she still does it...

I flip down the sun visor, and the keys tumble free, landing on my lap.

My mother can't do anything to hurt me now. She only has Vera. Neither of them can handle a gun, and there's no one left for her to manipulate. Without a Pakhan-in-waiting, she couldn't rally anyone to her cause if she tried.

The thought is some comfort. Dani and her family will be safe.

As for me, there's no way I can come back from this.

But I have to see Dani one more time, even if it costs my life.

23

DANI

"Slow down, Fyodor!"

Brutus is shouting, the panic clear in his voice. Mama leaps to her feet and runs for the door, flinging it open.

Papa's car is coming down the driveway far too fast. He's advancing on the gates, swerving as he gets nearer. Brutus stands in his way, waving his arms.

"Boss, stop!"

As the car gets closer, I see blood spattered over the hood. The windshield is shattered, and I'm amazed my father can drive the vehicle at all.

The passenger seat is empty.

Something is badly wrong. He's not slowing down.

"Fyodor!" my mother screams.

It looks like the car will smash into the gates, but at the last moment, it veers off to one side, hitting the garden wall.

Mama runs outside, with Mel and me behind her.

The hood is buckled. The car alarm is blaring, and as I get closer, I see the airbag. My father is slumped face-first into it.

He's not moving.

Brutus gets there before me. He picks through broken glass and tries to open the door, but it's too mangled. He reaches through the broken window and pulls my father up, setting him back against the seat.

"Papa," I sob.

His eyes are closed. There's a massive patch of blood on his shoulder, soaking through his jacket, and his face is so pale that I can see the veins in his temples. There's dried blood on his ear too.

Then I see it. His breath mists the air beneath his nose, and I nearly faint with relief.

"We need to get him inside," Brutus says. "Get something to carry him on, and we'll all take a corner."

Mel runs into the house, returning with a bed sheet. We lay it on the ground, and Mama and Brutus carefully lift Papa onto it.

The lounge has the most floor space, so we place him gently onto the rug in front of the fireplace. He's coming around now, grabbing at Mama's hands.

"Marta, my Marta…"

"Shh, *milaya*," she says, touching his face, "I'm here."

That's what Kal calls me. I wonder what—

"He tricked me," Papa whispers. "That fucking *truslivyy* piece of shit. Argh!" He convulses in pain as Brutus pulls his jacket away from the wound in his shoulder. "Fucking *warn* me if you're gonna do that!"

Brutus frowns. "The doctor will have to dig that out, Boss," he says. He goes to the drinks cabinet and returns with a bottle of vodka, handing it to Mama. "Here."

I want my father to tell us what happened, but I know the knowledge will destroy me. There's not much to be said. Kal isn't here. My father is badly hurt. And Vera told me a few things I can't ignore.

I know what Kal did. I only need to find out whether the father of my child is alive.

"Kal's dead, isn't he?"

My father isn't listening. He's reaching for the vodka.

"I need a drink."

"That's not what it's for," Brutus says, peeling my father's shirt off. "I need to clean the injury and patch it up." He nods at my mother, and she pours the vodka over the open wound. Papa grits his teeth and grunts, turning to me.

"Kal used you to get to me, Dani," he says. He's struggling to focus. "It was all planned out. His mother and brother followed us and tried to kill me, but I got away."

I thought I was prepared to hear it. But my heart wasn't ready.

Could Kal have looked at me the way he did, said those things, and not meant one bit of it?

It seems impossible, yet my father is telling me that the man I love conspired to have him killed and almost succeeded.

It's only now that I realize I was still holding onto hope. I wanted to believe that there was an explanation for all this, that Kal would return with my father and apologize for being controlling and evasive. That he'd take me in his arms and swear he'd never let the darkness consume him.

But he never even tried. It was all for fun, for show.

Even if Kal loved me, it wasn't enough. He wanted to destroy, seize, steal and kill, and I was just one more thing for him to possess.

"Oh, there's a fucking surprise!" Mel says from the hallway. She's at the front door, keeping watch. "Did you kill him, Papa?"

"I tried. Kal's brother shot me, and I ran him down with the car. He won't be walking away from that. But then I had to get away." He sighs and reaches for my hand. "If he comes back here, I *will* kill him."

"Fyodor, you won't be killing anybody," Mama says. "You're going to rest, and we'll get you a doctor to fix your shoulder."

Mel gives a yelp of shock. Brutus heads into the hallway, picking up his gun as he goes.

"What's the matter, Mel?" Mama says.

"It's Kal. He's back to finish the job."

I scramble to my feet and push past Brutus, running to the door. Mel grabs at me, but no force on Earth can stop me.

Kal is climbing over the wrecked car. He jumps over the wall just as I reach him.

"Dani," he says, "Listen—"

I didn't plan to do it. A white-hot searing rage powers through my muscles, and I pull my arm back, smashing my fist into Kal's chin.

I'm not strong enough to hurt him, but he wasn't expecting it. He stumbles backward, clutching his jaw.

"Stop," he says, holding a hand to fend me off. "Let me explain. Things aren't how they seem."

"No, you listen!" I scream. "I'm sick of hearing your voice lying to me. Tell me the truth!"

Brutus is at my side, his gun raised. I put my hand on top of it, pressing it down.

"Let me talk to him. I need some closure."

"I'm not making any promises," Brutus says, narrowing his eyes at me. "If this prick steps out of line, I will fucking shoot him. Otherwise, I'll leave him to your father."

I look at Kal.

"So Fyodor will be okay?" he asks.

"He needs a doctor and a good sleep, but he's survived worse," I reply. "Which is more than can be said for me. Why, Kal? Why did you drag me down to your level?"

"Not a day will pass where I don't ask myself that same question."

Kal looks broken. He seems weary and defeated, but his eyes are brighter than ever. I'm struck by an image of our child, a baby with the same cool blue gaze, and my rage disintegrates into a feeling of deep, agonizing sorrow.

This man was my everything.

Five minutes ago, as I held my father's hand, I believed Kal had lied to me and used me to make it easier for him to take control of our empire and our lives. He went from the love of my life to the very personification of betrayal in just one day.

Yet he's here. He just climbed over the wall in plain sight, with no plan, no nothing. Just like on the night he saved me from the fire…

"Answer my questions," I say. "Yes or no is enough."

He keeps his eyes on mine. It's as though he has nothing to offer but the truth, anyway. Surely he knew he was risking his life coming here?

"Okay, Dani. Ask away. I'm through with lying to you."

I take a deep breath.

"Did you and your family plot to burn down the gallery so that you could rescue me?"

"Yes."

It's like he punched me in the gut. It was hard to come to terms with the loss of my work when I thought it was a tragic accident, but this…

"Were you using me to get close enough to my father to kill him?"

Kal shifts his feet. "Dani, please..."

"Answer me!" I cry.

"Yes. At first."

The tears are flowing now. I don't care. I can't imagine I'll do anything other than cry for the rest of my life.

"You said you'd left your family. Was that bullshit? Were you in touch with them the whole time?"

"Yes, but—"

"Stop. Lies upon lies upon lies. Do you know what was true and what wasn't?"

"Yes, I fucking do!" Kal steps towards me, and I can see he's fighting back the tears too. Brutus snaps his gun back to eye level.

"Brutus," Kal says. "Please."

Mel is standing behind me.

"Fucking shoot him," Mel says. Brutus looks from her to me, and I shake my head.

"You see what you've done, Kal?" I ask. "It's years since anyone tried to hurt Papa. Before you came to us, our lives were peaceful. And then he trusted you, of all people, only for you to try to kill him." I jab my finger at him. "And I chose to fucking love you, only to find I have no idea who you are!"

"Neither do I."

Kal moves closer, and his eyes pull me toward him. He reaches for me, but I find some resolve and dodge his touch.

"I told you I'm rotten," he says. "I'm a bad guy, a sicko. I never thought there was a place for me in this world except for my mother's instrument of vengeance. For years, nothing else mattered. Until you."

On Kal's face, I see an expression I've seen before. This is how he looked at me when he asked me to marry him. When he bared his soul to me.

"At first, it was just sex. I only meant to toy with you. The plan was to kill your father and take his place, just as my stepfather tried and failed to do. But you changed me. You showed me a way out and gave me a reason to turn my back on everything I thought mattered."

I still believe in him.

God help me. I know I'm a fucking fool. But why else would he come back to me?

Mel is speaking.

"So what happened tonight?"

"My mother and Simeon must have tailed us somehow." Kal drops his face into his hands. "I don't know how I missed it. But they ambushed us, and Simeon knocked Fyodor out. While Idina tried to convince me to follow through with her plan, Fyodor came around and—"

A crash behind me. My father is striding unsteadily along the path, shirtless, with a fresh patch of gauze on his injured shoulder. Mama tries to hold him back, but he shoves her aside, and she stumbles to the ground.

I've never seen him do something like that to Mama.

Papa has his rifle in his hands.

24

KAL

"Leave us, Brutus," Fyodor says. "Take my wife and daughters inside. They don't need to see this."

Mel reaches her hand to Dani.

"Come on," she says. "It was all a fucking mirage, Dani. He was a figment of your imagination, a daydream. No good hanging onto fantasies."

Dani is still looking at me. I hold her image in my mind, knowing she may be the last thing I ever see.

Then she speaks.

"I am not leaving." She turns to her father with a steady, unwavering gaze. "Whatever happens now, I will witness it."

Brutus is shepherding Mel up the path, helping Marta to her feet as they go.

"Fyodor," I begin, "I came back because I had to at least ask for your forgiveness—"

"And you may have it."

I was ready to make my impassioned appeal for absolution, but now I don't know what to say next.

Fyodor fills in the silence. "I forgive you, Kal. How could you do any different? Conceived from a brutal, dehumanizing act of violence. Raised to be a bitter, twisted creature capable only of wreaking destruction and havoc on innocent people. And I was stupid enough to show some faith because I wanted to believe the chain could be broken."

"No, that's not how it is. Not anymore."

"Papa," Dani says. "Kal loves me for the person I am. The good you saw in him was real. Why would he be here, alone and unarmed, if he wasn't telling the truth?"

"You're a poor judge of character, Dani," Fyodor says. He doesn't look at her as he speaks but keeps his eyes on me. "I thought I knew people, but maybe I don't. You must get it from me."

"Mama told me whatever I believe will turn out to be true. I believe this man returned tonight because he wants to right this wrong." She shudders as she exhales, afraid to finish her thought. "Because we have our baby to think of."

Fyodor closes his eyes for a beat, then opens them again, glaring at me. He looks as though he has a thousand things he wants to say, but nothing comes out.

I'm stung by the realization that, for the first time, I'm losing a man I thought of as a father.

Fyodor raises the rifle. I freeze and fix my eyes on Dani, hoping her father will grant me a headshot and put me out of my misery.

"As I said, Kal," Fyodor says, advancing on me. "I forgive you. We will get past this and move forward. But I will *never* fucking forget. I will always remember the pain you wrought and how I allowed you to weasel your way into our lives. But mark my words. Dani's child will never know your fucking name, let only know *you*. You're no one."

I raise my hands. What's the point of anything now?

"Fuck it. Kill me if you must, Fyodor. I can't take any of it back. Without Dani and the baby, I have nothing."

I'm looking down the barrel of the rifle when Dani steps in front of it, facing her father.

"I won't let you do it, Papa," she says. "Just let him go."

"Get out of the way, Dani," Fyodor snarls. "You've done enough damage as it is."

She doesn't move a muscle.

"No. If you try and shoot Kal, I'll be in the way, and you'll have to risk killing me. Do you want your pound of flesh enough?"

Dani turns to me. "You'll go and never come back. Won't you?"

I want to say no, but I have no choice.

"I'll go, *milaya*."

I hope she sees it in my face, in my eyes.

I didn't do it. I've changed.

And I love you.

She turns away.

There's a long silence. Dani doesn't take her eyes off her father.

I admire her so much. She has the kind of strength and fortitude that I didn't know fucking existed.

Fyodor shoulders the rifle and walks past me, opening the gate.

"Get out of here," he says. "If you show your face again, you die."

∼

As I walk away towards the car, I don't look back. I can't.

Leaving Idina's home forever was a cakewalk compared to this. I had a love that was one in a million, and she'll have my baby. A child I won't know.

I'll never get the chance to be a good father. All I want is to be with Dani and raise our kid in a happy home. Give them an upbringing that's a million miles from my own.

Way back, when I realized my entire life's purpose and all the spoils were nothing compared to Dani's love, all I had to do was tell the fucking truth. I could have told her and risked her wrath, but no. I stalled, thinking I was smart and could make everyone around me bend to my will.

Look where that got me.

My family all said I was weak, and they were right.

Well, I'm free now. I could go anywhere. Do anything.

My bank account is still full of Erik's money. The inheritance that he refused to leave to Simeon and Vera, lest they think they mattered to him.

And me? Planted by force in the womb of a frightened young woman. It sickens me that Erik knew what happened to Idina - knew where I came from - and still treated her the way he did.

No wonder my mother and stepfather saw such potential in me to unleash hell on their enemies. They thought I was evil, right down to my DNA.

I think about everything Dani and I shared. We had so much to build on. She did all she could to dig out the good in me, and everything fell apart just when I started to believe I could overcome my past. I should have known better.

I drive to the ferry port and take a walk.

It was such a short time ago that Dani and I came here, but now it feels like I imagined it.

Years from now, when I'm still just as alone as I am now, I'll remember her eyes lighting up when she said yes to my proposal. The memory will always be there of her in her studio, paint on her cheek, as she told me we were having a baby.

My mind is struggling to process the total loss I'm experiencing. I have neither the familiar comfort of my shitty old life nor the warmth and hope of a bright future.

I just exist. Without Dani, without her love to light me up, I can already feel the cold creeping back inside me, freezing my heart. Maybe it's for the best.

I look out over the water at the boats, and the thought comes to me, ruthless as the chill wind that whips the ocean into choppy peaks.

I am the architect of my own misery.

25

DANI

As Kal disappears into the dark, my Papa falls to the ground.

"Help!" I cry. "Someone get out here, quick!"

Brutus wrenches the front door open and runs down the path with Mama behind him. For the second time this evening, we help Papa into the house.

As we pass the doorway to the lounge, I see my sister sitting on the window-ledge. I'm about to call out to her when Mama stops me.

"Leave her be," she says, with a little shake of her head. "Mel has had enough."

Papa's not unconscious this time, and we get him up to his bed without much difficulty. Mama pulls up a chair beside him.

"I'm sorry I pushed you," Papa says to Mama as she takes his hand. She rests his knuckles on her cheek.

I did that to Kal. I must have seen my parents do that before.

"It's okay, Fyodor," Mama whispers. "You were afraid for Dani. I know that. You never got over nearly losing Mel all those years ago."

"What?" I ask.

Mama sighs. "When Erik Antonov came and tried to take the empire by force, he and his cronies were routed, but not before Erik tried to kill Mel. That was why your father shot him."

"So it wasn't about the Bratva?"

"No." Mama rests her elbow on her knee, supporting her head in her hand. "It was about the *family*, Dani. That's all it's ever been about, and that's why we wanted so much to believe in Kal."

"*I* still believe in him, Mama."

The words are out before I can stop myself, but I don't want to take them back.

When my Papa had his rifle pointing at the man I love, I knew there was nothing I could do to de-escalate the situation, so I made him leave. It was the only way to prevent him from being murdered there and then.

But I no longer think he's a liar and a bastard.

He told me the truth when he told me he's a fucked-up, wounded guy with a freak on his back. He panicked out of a genuine desire to protect me, but he went about it all wrong, and I was so ready to see him through the lens of my prejudice.

At the first whiff of trouble, I hurled myself over the line and embraced fear, paranoia, and mistrust. I believed Kal must be using me because there are no good Bratva men, no happy Bratva wives. No love or respect between married couples in our world.

Yet my Papa was brought up in an abusive, loveless home, and he chose to turn away from it. He's an honorable man of true strength who loves my mother fiercely. He has never oppressed Mama, and Papa holds her counsel in the same high esteem as any of his advisors.

Now he's here, surrounded by people who love him, his adoring wife holding his hand.

And *he* is Bratva.

What a fucking fool I am.

I was so quick to judge Kal when I've been a victim of the same judgment my whole life.

Bratva princess. In need of protection. I can't do what I want. Naïve.

Like me, he knows how it feels to be defined by a role you can't escape and didn't ask for.

I should have realized that *he* might understand me better than anyone. Brutus comes into the room.

"I called your doctor. He'll be along soon, but he thinks you were running on adrenaline, and when that dumped out of your system, the blood loss and concussion caught up with you." He places a carafe of water on the nightstand. "You gotta rest up for now."

My father is trying to sit up.

"Dani," he croaks. "Come here, *dorogaya.*"

I sit on the bed beside him, opposite my mother. He lifts his hand to point at me, but it's as though his finger is made of lead, and he lowers it again.

"That was a foolish thing you did back there," he says, "but I know why you did it. You're in love with Kal and having his child. But you must understand - this was all just a way to get to me."

"You're wrong." I glance at Mama, but she won't meet my eyes. "I think he was about to tell you the truth when his family attacked you. He didn't know they were coming for you."

Papa is listening, but he says nothing.

"When all hell had broken loose, Kal *came back*. He could have left forever, but he returned, unarmed, to try and make amends." I touch my father's hand. "I think he *started* with a plan to use me, but everything changed."

Papa squeezes his eyes as though his head is hurting him, and I remember he's likely in great pain. He won't risk upsetting us by admitting it.

"I'm sorry this happened," I say. "If I thought it would have come to this, I'd never have let myself fall. But he does love me. I think you know it, too, but you can't let go of your fear."

Papa frowns. "Even if you're right, Kal is gone, and now I need to keep you safe. I let my guard down and look what happened."

Depraved Royals

He looks past me to Brutus. "Take Dani to her room. Confiscate her phone and override her door lock."

"No!" I cry, leaping to my feet. "Papa! You've never locked me in before!"

"I'm sorry," he says, "but I can't trust you not to do something dumb. Not anymore."

I look at my mother. She shakes her head slowly.

"You'll come around, Dani," she says. "In time, you'll see this is for the best."

Brutus takes my arm.

None of this would have happened if I hadn't fallen in love with the enemy.

∽

The door locks behind me, and I'm alone.

It's my childhood bedroom from back when we all still lived together. My posters are on the wall - not movie stars or boy bands, but art prints.

Hockney. Warhol. Pollock. All the modern art I love is tacked to the wall where I put it, back when I had freedom and blue skies above me.

I want that feeling back. I want to look into the world and see possibilities, opportunities, and a life.

But there's no life I want now that doesn't have Kal in it. He's the future I want. I understand now that he faced death just so he could give me the closure I needed. He left because I *told* him to go.

He respects me enough not to fight me, not to make my father kill him in front of me.

And he loves me enough to leave.

The damage here is done. My father will never come to terms with what happened, so I'll never be free again.

I open my bedroom window and look outside.

Brutus no longer guards the gate. With Kal gone and Simeon dead, there are no more Antonovs to fear. Idina can't hurt us on her own.

Instead, he's guiding my sister to the limo.

"Mel!" I cry. "Don't go. Get Papa to let me out of here!"

"I tried," she says, throwing her arms in the air. "He won't listen to anyone. I can't cope anymore. I'm going home."

I watch the limo pull out of the gates, creeping past the mangled remains of the Alfa, and I feel utterly alone.

I head to my dresser and pick up my old jewelry box. I wonder if...

Yes. Right there, in the secret drawer, a roll of twenty-dollar bills. Mel went through a phase of stealing from me when we were younger; this was my best hiding place.

I look outside the house, wondering if I have the guts to try something...

To the right of my window is a downspout. It's painted cream to match the plaster, but I can see it clearly.

I climb onto the window-ledge and swing my legs to the outside, tapping my heels on the wall. I perch there for a moment, steeling myself.

I can do it.

I shift along the ledge until I can reach the downspout. The gap behind it is wide enough to get a hand behind it. I reach my right foot out until I can tuck my toe onto a bracket that holds the pipe to the wall.

Come on. One big push is all it'll take.

I push off the ledge. I start to slip, but momentum keeps me going, and I wrap my body around the downspout, locking my feet behind it.

With a few slips and stifled shrieks, I slide from bracket to bracket until I reach the ground. I collapse onto my knees, waiting for my breathing to stabilize before getting to my feet.

That's it. I'm outta here.

∼

I walk for a while until I start to see cars. As I try to flag down a cab, I wonder where I'm gonna go.

How will I find Kal? I don't know where to start, and I can't do anything now. Dawn is breaking, it's bitterly cold, and all I have is a few dollars and the clothes on my back.

This is dumb. My father will pick me up in no time, and what then?

I decide to hide out somewhere until I can figure it out. Maybe I can reach Vera somehow. She's a bitch, but what does she have left now? She might know where Kal would hide out. I'll even go to Idina if I have to.

A cab slows down beside me and pulls to a stop. I jump in the back.

"Where you headed?" the driver asks.

"I need a motel that's as far from here as you'll take me for..." I count my money quickly, "...say, thirty dollars?"

"No problem. I know a place."

26

DANI

The motel has a diner attached to it, and both seem quiet. Within five minutes of arriving, I have a room.

I lie on the bed and stare at the ceiling, wondering what I'm gonna do.

Can I turn my back on my family? If I have to, yes. But the thought is like a dagger in my heart.

My father has resources, and, of course, he'll find me pretty quickly. If I somehow reach Kal, he'll instantly be in danger because anyone working for my father would know what happened and likely shoot Kal on sight.

I love him. I have to find him.

The handle on the door rattles.

I jump to my feet. Scanning the room, I spot a heavy glass ashtray and grab it.

"What do you want?" I yell.

"Dani! Let me in!"

I drop my makeshift weapon and run for the door.

I can't believe it's him. With the entire world to run to, he's here.

The deadbolt is sticking. Finally, I slide it free and fling open the door.

Kal's eyes are tinged with red, and his skin is sallow. But he never looked better to me. I was afraid I'd never see him again.

He leans against the doorjamb, letting out a sigh of relief.

"Dani. You're alright. I was afraid something had happened to you." He looks around. "Why are you here?"

"What the hell?" I ask. "Kal, why the fuck are you here? How did you find me?"

Kal massages his forehead with his fingertips, avoiding my eyes. "You're not gonna like it, *milaya*." He reaches for me, and I'm enveloped in his arms, my cheek against his chest. I shudder as he reaches beneath my hair and touches the back of my neck.

"That tickles. What are you—"

He's holding up a small patch of clear plastic that looks like a band-aid.

"I was tracking you," he says. "I was worried my brother would try to kidnap you, or you'd just run away, seeing as you weren't listening to me."

I shove him away. "And when did you put that on me?"

"In your apartment, when we were fighting. Just before I took you to your parent's house."

"Kal, who even has something like that handy?"

He shrugs. "Me. I'm just that kind of guy. Part of my *Spetsnaz* field kit I carry around."

"I forgot about that. You never said whether you were in the Special Forces."

"And I never will. Now, are you gonna let me in?"

We enter the room, and I close the door, bolting it again.

"What are we gonna do?" I ask. "I can't just run away with you."

"Yes, you can. Fyodor has his ways and means, but so do I. We have the plane; we have money. He's in no shape to be running around looking for you, anyway."

"Kal, he has people who will scour the Earth for me if he tells them to. Haven't you learned anything about true loyalty? And that's not the point. I love my family. And you love them too."

Kal wraps his hands around my waist and pulls me to him, lowering his lips to my neck. I shiver as he runs his tongue over my skin.

"I love you, Dani. More than anything. All this shit can wait because right now, I want you."

"What, in a bed?" I say. "That's novel, for us at least."

He grips my ass with one hand, holding me to him, while his other hand rakes through my hair, grabbing a handful and pulling gently.

"Have you somehow hidden some kinky accessories in here?" I ask.

Kal laughs against my neck. "Nope. And it's not about that, not this time."

He lets go of my hair and cups my ass with both hands. I give a brief shriek of delight as he picks me up, my legs wrapping around his waist. His cock presses against my sex, and I grind against him, making him moan.

"You can keep doing that," he says. He carries me to the bed and lays me on my back, standing back to look at me.

"Hey." I sit up on my elbows. "Get out of your clothes."

Kal raises his eyebrows. "As you command."

As he strips off his jacket and shirt, I notice a finger-width scar stretching about six inches, starting at his hipbone. He sees me looking and points at it.

"That?" He removes his pants, sits beside me, and reaches for my waistband, tugging my leggings down and off. "Forget it."

I pull my tank top over my head, and he sighs at the sight of my naked body. My nipples stand proudly, waiting for his attention.

Kal pushes me backward and settles between my legs. His erection throbs against my inner thigh as he lowers his weight onto me.

He kisses me, and I know for sure. This man loves me.

His mouth moves naturally against mine, our lips caressing one another. I nuzzle the hollow of his neck. His fingertips graze my flank, stimulating my nipple with his thumb.

"What do you want?" he murmurs. "I'll do anything. Tell me."

"I want you everywhere at once," I sigh. "I want your tongue on my pussy, your hands all over me, and your cock..." he ducks his head to lap at my nipple, and the words die on my lips.

"You want my cock in every luscious hole, don't you?" Kal pulls away and kneels between my legs, grinning at my flushed face. He slides my panties over my knees and tosses them aside, rubbing the length of his middle finger through my slit. "You're so fucking sexy, Dani. Always hot for me. You want me in here?"

I nod. He grins and presses his fingertip onto my clit. The tiny movements are enough to make my eyes roll to the back of my head.

"But I also want you to tease me until I can't take it anymore," I say.

"This indecisiveness isn't getting us anywhere."

He continues to play with my pussy, stroking his cock as he does so. "I need you, Dani. It's been an absolute cunt of a day, and I got a lot of tension I need to work off." He grips his cock, rubbing the head against my clit as he pushes a finger inside me. "Left up to me, I'll flip you over and let the pillow drown out your screams as I fuck you hard enough to smash the headboard through to the next room."

I laugh despite myself. He's driving me crazy.

"Okay. I'll turn over, but I want your mouth on me. Then you can rail me to your heart's content."

He grins. "You got it. They say relationships are about compromise, right?"

I roll onto my front, and before I even finish getting comfortable, I feel Kal's hands parting the cheeks of my ass. He spears my asshole with his tongue, and I gasp with delight. It's so sensitive, and every lick feels sublime.

"I wanna put my cock in here," he says, "but not now. I'm gonna open you up just a little."

Still holding my buttocks, he slips his thumb between my juicy pussy lips, dragging my wetness up and onto my asshole. He moves it around, making me slippery. I groan as he presses his thumb into me, his fingertips squeezing my flesh as he grips me tight.

"You're so tight." He slides his thumb in and out, and I clutch at it, my pussy spasming with jealousy. "Fucking dirty girl, you are. I'm a lucky bastard."

I'm beside myself with joy. All the pressure and loss we both have to face are forgotten. There's only us.

If my pussy has a mind of its own, it's losing it. I feel almost painfully empty, and I can't take it anymore.

"Kal, just do what you want," I say, pushing back onto him. His cock is like a firebrand on my ass, and he presses against my entrance, earning a fresh gush of juice.

"Touch yourself," he says. "I won't pretend this is gonna last long. All you have to do is take me, but I know you want to come too. You can do that for me, can't you?"

He slips inside me, and I hiss through my teeth. His girth is a challenge, no matter how wet I am. I reach beneath me, finding my clit as he leans his weight onto me, pushing his cock into the hilt.

"Oh fuck. There's nothing better, I swear." Kal seems to be talking more to himself than me. "I'll never get enough of you."

He pushes the thumb in my asshole even deeper, getting a firm grip on my buttock. He leans over my back, his other hand snaking around my throat. I feel the bones in his fingers as he squeezes my neck just firmly enough for me to shudder at the sensation.

"You'd better be ready," he says, but he doesn't wait for an answer. He moves his hips, pulling almost entirely out of me before sliding deep inside me again. His thumb only magnifies the sensation in my ass, and as my pussy squeezes his shaft, my ass contracts too.

Kal moves his thumb in time with his thrusts. He leans close to my ear.

"Ever felt this good before?" he asks.

How he thinks I have the capacity to answer him, I don't know. He's driving me towards my orgasm, my fingers on my clit helping me along.

He slows down. "Answer."

"No," I gasp. He seems satisfied with this, and his movements gather pace once again.

"Well, get used to it. I'll give you everything I've got, and that will be enough. You belong to me." He slams his cock into me so hard that I nearly smack into the headboard. "Don't you?"

"Yes." My core is heating now, and the pleasure is radiating through my body. "Yes, Kal! Just keep fucking me!"

He growls and pulls me upright, his hand still wrapped around my throat. I cry out as he removes his thumb from my ass so he can grip my waist with both hands, bouncing me on him. His hot breath in my ear as he fucks me tips me over the edge, and my pussy gushes as I clutch and shudder all over his cock. He slams me onto him and holds me in place, emptying into my pussy.

We don't move for a minute. I lean against him, and he wraps his arms around my body to support me. The bed sheets are soaked with our fluids, and we're both covered in sweat.

I start to feel cold and disentangle myself from Kal's embrace, pulling on my clothes. He takes my cue and does the same, but as he's buttoning his shirt, I see the scar again.

"Tell me what happened to you," I say, gesturing at the silvery line streaking his skin.

"It's a burn," he says. "My mother threw a baking tray at me when it just came out of the oven. She never told me why. I tried to move, but it landed on top of me, edge down, and burned my t-shirt onto my skin. I was eight."

He seems to be miles away, and I'm heartsore. The man I love carries such a painful burden. These memories will haunt him forever.

"I understand why you want to make a new start," I say. "I really do. But it's gonna be hard for me to come to terms with leaving my family behind."

Kal stands beside me and takes my hand.

"I won't force you," he says. "You ran away, and we found each other. But all bullshit aside, Dani - I won't hold you back. Reality may yet be too much. If you want to go home and live your life, I'll provide for you and the baby and ask only that you don't shut me out completely. I love you, but I won't hurt you to keep you by my side."

"No." I kiss him. "I'm staying with you, whatever comes. If my father hunts us down and we have to live on the run forever, that's how it is. Some scars run too deep to heal properly, so we live with them."

∼

I smile at the waitress as she places our food in front of us.

"Thanks, doll," Kal says. He picks up his burger. "So, where shall we go?"

"I don't know." I stir my drink with the straw. "Any thoughts?"

"You told me you wanted to go to Paris. Pick up that lecture program at the Sorbonne."

"I guess."

I want my life with Kal, and I'm confident I'm making the right decision. If I leave the city quickly - the country, even - then by the time Papa finds out where I am, I'll be far out of his sphere of control. Launch my art career in Europe,

Florence, maybe? I never considered it before because Papa wouldn't have wanted me to be far from home for so long. Now it doesn't matter.

A family enters the diner. The parents are wrangling a mischievous toddler, a little girl. Her father is laughing as his daughter tries to climb up his leg. Behind them is an older couple, and from the resemblance, I'd say they are the child's maternal grandparents. Grandma is scolding the toddler good-naturedly, coaxing her into a booth and distracting her with the puzzles on the back of the kid's menu.

It's not until Kal touches my arm that I realize I'm crying. The tears have puddled on my plate, and my fries are soggy.

"Fuck it," Kal says. "I'm not letting this happen. We're going home. Both of us."

27

KAL

I'm standing in front of the house I thought I'd never return to, with Dani at my side.

"Are you sure about this?" she asks.

I nod. "Idina is grieving my brother, and so am I, although in many ways, I've been grieving him for years. She has only my sister and me, and I won't help her fulfill her dreams of killing your father, so she may be in a reflective mood. Who knows?" I sigh. "But it's gotta be worth a try. My mother used to frighten the shit out of me, but not anymore."

I no longer have my key, so I ring the doorbell. It's not Idina but Vera who opens it.

"Well, if it isn't the prodigal son," she says. "Why are you here? Come to kill me too?"

"Simeon died because our mother put him up to a job he couldn't do. For an outside chance of getting what she wanted, she fucked around and found out. I warned her and you he couldn't do it."

Vera stands aside to let me in, and it's only then that she notices Dani behind me.

"Oh, what the fuck?" Vera says, gesturing at Dani. "You had to bring her along? What good do you think that's gonna do?"

I take Dani's hand and pull her into the hallway. Something looks different, and then I notice.

The walls are covered in photos. Pictures I've never seen before. My siblings and I, at the beach, school sports days, and the park. Smiling but still looking somewhat uncomfortable. And a few taken at the Pushkin home, Erik and Idina standing with Fyodor and Marta. My mother is pregnant in some of them, and she's holding me in one. It's bizarre to see.

Vera sees me looking and scowls.

"You think there's no good in her, but there is," she says. "She's heartbroken, Kal, just like I said she would be. She wants to remember the happy times in her life."

Dani laces her fingers through mine. She sees my expression and knows I'm struggling.

"Tell her I want to talk to her," I say to Vera. "There's a way through this for all of us, and she can look forward to good times instead of clinging to the past. But she's gonna have to eat humble pie with a side of crow to get there."

Vera shrugs and goes upstairs. I hear her talking to Idina.

"So what are you proposing to do?" Dani asks.

"I want her to come to Fyodor, tell him the truth, and ask for his forgiveness. I believe he'll give it. Maybe she'll be a proper mother to me for the first time in her life. And I'll be redeemed to your family and, hopefully, pardoned for the shit I *did* do."

"It's *me* who you need to beg forgiveness from." Dani narrows her eyes at me. "When I saw you, I was too relieved to pick a fight, but I haven't forgotten what you did to my art."

"Me neither. I never will, *milaya*. You have that over me for the rest of our lives."

Vera appears at the top of the stairs.

"So she's willing to speak to you both," she says. "Fuck knows why. You best come up here."

We walk up the stairs and into my mother's room.

She usually keeps it tidy, but everything looks disheveled, and her bed is unmade. The wastepaper bin is full of burned photos, some of which are still mostly intact. I pick one up and see it's a wedding portrait of her and Erik. His eyes have been burned out with cigarettes.

"He hated me, and I hated him," Idina says. She's sitting on her window seat, a mug of her perennial mint tea in hand. "It's that simple." She looks past me and gives Dani a strangely jovial wave. "Hello, Danica. How are you feeling, dear?"

"I... I'm okay," Dani says, sounding uneasy. She's picking up on the vibes too. "Not as sick as I was yesterday."

"Hmm." Idina sips her tea. "Don't loiter, children. Come and sit."

Dani takes the chair, and I put the picture down before sitting beside my mother on the window seat.

When I saw her last, she was determined to tear me down, and she didn't care how crazy she seemed.

Now it's as though my mother has had a lobotomy.

She's smiling beatifically at me and keeps stealing glances at Dani. Not a single iota of her usual cattiness, no bitchy asides, and, given the circumstances, no screamed accusations of murder and betrayal. It's unexpected, and I don't know how to respond. I was ready to meet her rage with an appeal to her ego.

Only you can help me, that's what I was going to say. *You have all the power here. Please help me. Save me.*

It's a relief that I don't have to do that. Idina looks at me like she did when she still thought I was her golden child.

"I'm so glad you came to see me," she says. "You and Danica. Is everything alright, my son? Do you need me?"

Her eyes are so wide and pleading. It's grotesque, in a way.

Vera loiters in the doorway. An expression of utter confusion has replaced her customary sour one. I search her eyes, but she shakes her head slightly.

She doesn't get it, either.

I take a deep breath.

"Idina, you need to come and see Fyodor and tell him I didn't set him up."

"I don't think he'll be pleased to see me, Kal," she says. "He doesn't like me at all."

I feel like I'm going insane. Sitting in the morning sunshine with her greying hair braided down her back, tea in hand, this woman looks like a benign spirit. She's talking about Fyodor as if it's all been some silly misunderstanding. Didn't she throw things at these very walls, screaming his name and calling him a cunt and a bastard and every other profanity that came into her mind?

"He needs to know that I didn't have any part in the ambush that almost got him killed. I want to marry Dani and be a part of a happy family. You can have that too, but you will have to admit your role and say that you're sorry."

Idina closes her eyes.

"Okay, I will," she murmurs. "I accept the cards I've been dealt. Maybe it's justice, after a fashion. But Simeon didn't need to die."

"You must make your peace with that, not me. I won't carry guilt. It's not my burden to bear."

"I accept that."

She stands up and places her cup on the table. The wedding photo is there, and she picks it up.

"Erik never let me forget that I was ruined," say says. "He said no one but him would ever love me because I was having the child of a monster. But he was obsessed with you, Kal, even after he and I had two children of our own. He was sure you would be a soulless creature, capable of seizing power and prestige he couldn't gain for himself." She looks at the photo a moment longer before dropping it into the wastepaper bin. "All that is over now. I have nothing left. So I may as well face up to it and take my punishment."

Dani speaks up.

"My Papa won't punish you. He isn't like that. He's just tired and wants this to be over." She stands and takes a step toward my mother. "We were a family. We can be again. There's so much to look forward to, and I hope you'll be there with us. Vera too."

There's a gasp from the doorway, but I don't look at my sister. I fix my eyes on Idina.

In theory, this is going far better than I could have dared to hope. I haven't had to convince my mother of anything - she seems to have started down the same path I did.

Is she seeing what I saw? Does she know how much we all hurt me with this bullshit?

Idina smiles as though she's had an epiphany. Maybe she is learning.

Dani introduced me to optimism. She dares to believe in the best outcomes in life, so perhaps I can do the same.

"I'll come with you," Idina says, "and talk to Fyodor. If he gives me his forgiveness, I'll bring the whole sad story to an end."

28

DANI

We arrive at my home. Kal, Idina, Vera and me.

I never imagined this would happen. The three surviving Antonovs. One to beg forgiveness, one to atone alongside her mother, and the third?

He went from my hated enemy to the man I would kill for.

I haven't been able to warn my parents that I'm bringing company. I don't think they would have taken it well, anyway. As we get out of the car, I see the gates are open, and Brutus isn't there.

"He'll be out looking for me," I say to Kal. "Papa is incapacitated, so all his people will be helping with the search."

Idina speaks. "We couldn't have taken the Pushkin Bratva by force after all, could we?"

I turn and stare at her, frowning. "What do you mean?"

"My plan depended on the notion that your father's supposedly loyal associates would switch allegiance as soon as they realized there was a new Pakhan. It never occurred to me they were so committed to Fyodor. They'd have ripped Kal to pieces for his insolence."

"Jesus, Idina," Kal says. "You're right, but why fucking mention it now? Let it go."

As we walk up the path to the door, Kal looks troubled.

"What's the matter?" I whisper.

"This feels wrong." He glances over his shoulder at his mother and sister. "The thought of them even being in your house makes me feel sick to my stomach. Maybe this is a mistake."

"She came here of her own volition, Kal," I say. "Give her a chance. All she needs to do is clear your name; if that's all we get, it's better than the alternative. She can't hurt us anymore."

Mama is halfway down the stairs as I turn my key in the lock. She screams and runs to the door when she realizes it's me.

"Dani!" She throws her arms around me, talking a mile a minute. "You scared us so much! Only your father and I are here. Brutus and Mel are out searching for you. The doctor got the bullet out of Papa's shoulder and—"

Mama falls silent. I feel her go still and stiff as she sees who is behind me.

"Hello, Marta," Idina says. "It's been a while."

Mama looks at her for a long moment before turning to me.

"You ran away only to find our enemies and bring them to our door? Why would you do this?"

Kal stands at my side. Mama glares at him, and he touches her arm gently. She pulls it away.

"Please, Marta." Kal tilts his head at Idina and Vera. "They're all I have left. I had nothing to do with the attack on Fyodor, but that doesn't mean I'm blameless in all this. I brought my mother here because she wants to tell him the truth and ask his forgiveness."

"And you?" Mama looks Kal in the eye. "What you want, Mikhail?"

"Dani." He wraps his arm around my waist, his hand resting protectively on my stomach. "I want her. She's everything. Whatever I have to do to make it right, I'll do it, even if I take the rest of my life. For her and our baby."

Mama and Kal regard each other for a few seconds, and something passes between them that doesn't need to be said.

"Alright," Mama says. She turns her attention to Idina and Vera. "Come inside. I'll tell Fyodor you're here. But if he says you must leave, you're all going, except for Dani. Understood?"

Idina nods, and when Vera sees it, she nods too.

We wait as Mama remonstrates with my father. His delight at my return rapidly switches to anger, his voice rising.

I can't hear him too well, but the occasional word is clear.

Traitors. Murderers. Twisted. Sick.

I watch Idina's face as she listens, but her expression is neutral. Her flat affect is weird, but I guess she's nervous.

Mama comes downstairs.

"We can go to him," she says. "You Antonovs need to keep well back from Fyodor's bed unless he says otherwise." She turns to me. "He's doing this for you, Dani. He's injured and vulnerable, but I don't believe you'd do something like this if you weren't sure. I told him that, and he's willing to talk."

I look at Kal. He has his heart set on this working out, and he's right - it's our last shot. So I have to project confidence and back him up.

But I'm not as confident as I was. There's a gnawing pain in my stomach, but it's not morning sickness. It's anxiety.

Get a hold of yourself, Dani.

What do I know anyway? Kal is okay with this, and he knows Idina best.

Papa doesn't look as unwell as he did yesterday. He sits up in his bed, a cup of coffee beside him on the nightstand.

We all file in awkwardly, like kids who've been sent to see the head teacher. Papa reaches for me, and I sit on the chair beside him.

Idina and Vera stand at the foot of the bed. Papa stares at them in silence.

Eventually, he speaks.

"Vera Antonov," he says, cocking his head. "You look like your father, which means you also kinda look like me."

Vera shifts her weight from one foot to the other. "Yeah," she says. "W-w-weird."

I glance at Kal to see him staring slack-jawed at his sister. She didn't stammer when she came here and said all those horrible things to me. What's going on?

Papa doesn't comment on it. "I'm your Uncle Fyodor," he says, pointing at his face. "I wish we were meeting under better circumstances, *dorogaya*."

I don't know how to feel about him calling her 'sweetheart,' but I don't think he gave it a thought. The effect on Vera is palpable, though. Tears spring to the corners of her eyes, and I wonder if anyone has ever called her by an affectionate pet name in her entire life.

Papa's eyes slide over to Idina's. He holds her gaze, but when he speaks, it's not her he's addressing.

"Kal, you give me your word first," he says, "because, despite everything that happened, I still think it might be worth something. My Dani says you love her. Do you?"

Kal's voice is solid and sure.

"Yes, I do."

"Are you and your family here to end this?"

Idina answers.

"Yes, Fyodor, we are." She moves closer to my father's bed, but he doesn't object. "I'm done with all this. I want it to be over."

Papa beckons her with his finger, and Idina stands beside my father's bed, opposite where I'm sitting. Mama stands behind me, her hand on my shoulder. As Idina sits at the foot of the bed, Mama and I both draw a tight, nervous breath.

"What have you come here to say?" Papa asks.

Idina glances behind her at Kal. He raises his eyebrows and nods his head at Fyodor. She turns back and begins.

"I raised Kal with only one goal - to kill you and steal your empire, as Erik intended. When Kal met Dani, he saw she wanted him and felt he could orchestrate a way to get close to you through her. He and his siblings planned to burn down the gallery on the night of Dani's exhibition so that Kal could rescue her. He knew when he said he'd abandoned us, you would feel obliged to accept him into your home."

"A cunning scheme," Papa says. "I'm impressed. Go on."

Idina smiles. It doesn't extend far or last long. "He *meant* to kill you. But Dani showed him what love means, and he saw the world, and his family, very differently. Kal turned his back on his destiny, all for *love*.

"So Simeon and I watched until we saw our chance, followed you to the parking garage, and you know the rest. Kal had nothing to do with it." Her voice cracks. "You killed my boy, Fyodor."

Papa frowns. "Your husband, my brother, tried to shoot Mel when she was just a little girl for no reason other than spite. He would have brutally murdered a child for nothing. I killed him to prevent that, and I killed Simeon in self-defense. What would you have me do?"

Idina pulls her jacket around her, crossing her arms over it. "I have to live with the deaths of *two* family members, and now my oldest son has chosen you. You still have everything you always had." She sniffs. "But I guess it's all my fault, isn't it?"

Kal's head whips to look at his mother. He moves a little to see her face, his eyes scanning as though he's looking for something.

He's panicking. *Why?*

Idina is still talking.

"I came here to make amends, Fyodor. To bring the whole sorry business to a close. Do *you* have anything to say?"

"Fine." My father sits up a little straighter, leaning forward. He holds Idina's gaze as he speaks. "I'm sorry you lost your husband and your son. I'm sorry you haven't lived the life you feel you were due. And I wish it had all happened another way. But I'm glad the next generation is doing all they can to bridge the divide. The future is bright, yes?"

Idina sighs.

"Yes, it is. Because there will be no Antonov-Pushkin brat!"

Idina hurls herself across my father's bed, pinning him down.

Time slows to a crawl. I see Idina's arm rise in the air.

She has something in her hand.

I try to get to my feet. Moving backward, I crash into Mama, and she hits the floor hard.

Kal is reaching for his mother, his eyes wild.

"Mama!" Vera wails. "No! Don't, please!"

Idina reaches for me. A flash of brightness, and I feel a searing pain in my abdomen. I look down to see blood already staining my clothes. My head spins, and the walls rush past me as I fall to the floor.

Blood everywhere.

Idina Antonov's face before me, her eyes bulging.

I try to move away, pushing my feet out to fend her off, but my heels can't get any purchase on the slippery floor.

She's gonna kill me.

29

KAL

Idina swings her knife with enough force to almost hurl herself off the bed, but not quite.

Marta grabs Dani beneath her arms, dragging her away from my mother's flailing limbs. With an almighty heave, Fyodor lifts her legs and pushes her off him, and she slides off the bed and thuds to the ground, screaming maniacally as she goes.

"You fucking bastard Pushkins! I swear I'll carve that baby right out of her—"

With a wet, strangled yelp, Idina's voice cuts off.

I can't see what's happening. Then Vera claps her hand to her mouth.

"Oh dear God," she says.

I drop to my knees beside Marta. She's cradling Dani in her arms. Her clothes are thick with blood, her stomach and thighs soaked. I can't see where it's coming from.

I look around, trying to gauge how much blood she's lost, and I realize that it's mixing. Idina's is different - it has that thick, dark arterial quality that is only seen in people who rapidly bleed to death.

She fell on her knife.

The blade sliced cleanly through her jugular, the blood pumping only for a few seconds before ebbing away. Her eyes are open but blank, her wrathful expression frozen on her face.

My mother died as she lived. Consumed by hatred and twisted by trauma. She could have chosen a different path, but even when she was given a second chance, she squandered it, preferring to hold onto her pain.

I'm not going to make the same mistake.

"Hold on, Dani," I say, pressing my forehead to hers. She's whimpering, and I kiss her between her eyes. "Just hold on."

∼

Fyodor and Marta are waiting outside.

The obstetrician sets up the ultrasound machine.

I'm wracked with worry.

Dani is lying on her bed. She's so pale, the hollows of her eyes purple. She looks exhausted and so afraid.

I did this.

I brought my mother into her home in a last-ditch attempt to make amends, never suspecting she'd do something so utterly unhinged. I should have listened to my gut and not let Dani's hope and faith in me blind me to the danger.

When Idina said 'It's all my fault,' I fucking *knew*. That's what she used to say sarcastically before launching into one of her rants about how, in fact, nothing was her fault. How everyone conspired against her. How she was unappreciated, unloved, and unwanted.

The obstetrician powers up the doppler wand.

"The wound to your abdomen is superficial," she says, "and the closure adhesive will hold it for a few days until it heals. But you fell hard, and the cramps you've been getting worry me."

"They worry me, too," Dani replies.

She's trying so hard to stay calm, but her hand trembles in mine. I'm lost in admiration for her. Her world has fallen apart several times over in less than twenty-four hours, and here we are, waiting to see whether we get to keep our souls intact. But she's keeping it together.

Me? I'm fucking losing it.

The obstetrician moves the doppler around, pressing it to Dani's lower abdomen. She moves around a little, pushing a little harder.

"Sorry, Dani. I know it hurts where the wound is. Bear with me."

A minute passes.

Nothing.

The obstetrician squeezes gel onto Dani's stomach. No one says anything as she glides the transducer over her skin.

The image window is surrounded by lines of text that mean nothing to me, but I know that the picture needs to have more than what it shows right now. A featureless black, peppered with the occasional flurry of static.

Dani is crying now.

The obstetrician keeps moving the transducer. "Give it a minute," she says.

Dani and I stare at the screen. She's muttering under her breath.

"Please. Please, not this, not after everything we've been through…"

A flare of light on the screen. The obstetrician freezes, pressing harder. A whitish patch appears on the screen.

Dani draws a sharp breath, her hand squeezing mine.

At the center of the bubble is a flicker of movement. With a twist of her wrist, the obstetrician brings the shape into sharper focus, and the movement stabilizes into a rapid flutter. She sighs and grins broadly.

"Oh, *there* you are, little one."

I drop my head into my hand.

"Is everything okay?" Dani asks. "Does it seem alright?"

"It's fine, as far as I can tell."

The obstetrician is pointing at the screen, showing us all the incomprehensible arrangements of pixels. I'm half-listening, but I only have eyes for Dani. Her face is shiny from her tears, but her smile lights up the entire room.

The obstetrician is wiping the gel from Dani's skin.

"Will you go and speak to my parents?" Dani asks. "I just want to talk a couple of things over with the doctor."

∼

When I open the door, I nearly walk straight into Fyodor, who is pacing up and down the landing. Marta is sitting on the floor, leaning against the wall.

"Everything is fine," I say. "Baby is doing well, and Dani's stomach injury isn't too bad. It bled a lot, but now that it's patched up, it's no big deal."

Fyodor and Marta both look ready to pass out with relief, but they are smiling.

We go downstairs and into the lounge, where Mel is sitting with Vera. She's gently trying to coax her into eating some toast.

In the couple of hours since it all went down, my sister has barely spoken a word because she's stammering again. It breaks my heart to hear it after all these years.

All Vera wants is love, just like me. I haven't explained a thing to the Pushkins, and yet they are being kind to her. They seem to understand, somehow, and I'm reminded of just how much of our trauma is shared.

"How are you feeling, sis?" I ask.

Vera looks up at me. "I-I'm coping. B-b-but I feel t-terrible. I should have s-s-stopped her."

"Dani isn't badly hurt. The baby is fine."

Marta speaks. "And you can stay here with us for as long as you want, Vera. You need someone to take care of you."

Vera squeezes her eyes closed, fat tears running down her cheeks.

"I'm so s-sorry. For everything. I d-don't know why I let Idina d-do this to you."

"She did it to *you* first," Mel says. "It's not your fault you were raised by a narcissist. You've got a long way to go, but you're family too, not just Kal. We'll help you."

I kneel down so I can see Vera's face.

"You don't have to be that frightened little girl from now on," I say. "They grow jasmine here, Vera. You can be the person you really are, even if it takes a while to get there."

Vera leans forwards and rests her forehead on my chest. I wrap my arms around her, and for the first time in many years, I'm hugging my sister. I'm so fucking glad.

"Let's not hurt each other anymore," she whispers.

"No way."

Dani is at the front door, saying goodbye to the obstetrician. She closes the door and limps into the lounge, frowning when she sees Vera crying.

I give Vera a last squeeze and go to Dani.

"She's got a long way to go," I say. "It's been a real rollercoaster, and she doesn't know how to feel about losing Idina. Neither do I."

Fyodor puts a hand on my shoulder.

"It's gonna take time, son." He smiles fondly at Dani, chucking her under her chin. "But you have the love of a wonderful woman, and that's a damn good start."

30

KAL

One week later...

I watch the coffins as they descend into the furnace.

It's a surreal feeling. I expected to be more upset or angry, but now I'm just numb.

Vera has good days and bad. She nearly didn't make it today, but she's here, and she's crying. It's a sight I haven't seen in years. I'm holding her hand, and Dani has her arm around Vera's shoulder.

"It's okay," Dani murmurs. "Let it go now."

"I never thought I'd see this day," Vera says. "My mother hurt me so much, but I never wished her dead. And Simeon? I always thought there was hope for him. I really did."

It took a lot of money and effort to track down Simeon's body and even more to hush it all up. The short version is that Idina left the parking garage and never returned, leaving the broken body of her youngest son alone on the cold concrete. He was found eventually and shipped off to a morgue, where he was marked as a John Doe and left alone, waiting out the statutory ninety-six-hour waiting period. If Fyodor didn't have hospital orderlies on his payroll, my brother might have been embalmed and sent to a medical school somewhere.

As it was, we got to him in time, and mother and son are being cremated side by side.

There was some debate about what to do with the bodies. Fyodor wanted to bury them in the Pushkin family plot, but I didn't feel they earned the privilege, so we asked the women to adjudicate. In the end, Marta thought it was most appropriate to hold a respectful cremation ceremony and then leave it to Vera to decide what to do with the ashes.

Fyodor, Marta, and Mel are standing behind me, Fyodor's hand on my shoulder. I'm taking strength from him. He has it to spare.

"You'll be Pakhan, my son," he says. "Ironic. Everything Idina wanted was right there in front of her."

I shake my head. "You're wrong, Fyodor. I spent years promising to do whatever would make her happy, but it was futile. She wanted to make everyone else feel her pain, and nothing would have been enough. She was a toxic, twisted mess, but she didn't dare face up to it."

"It wasn't her fault," Marta says. "Idina needed help. I told her this many years ago, and she never forgave me for it. But you couldn't have done more than you did, Kal. You broke the chain, and you should be proud."

The coffins have disappeared, and there's no more to be said. We drift out into the chapel courtyard and through the archway that leads to the graveyard.

The Pushkin plot isn't only for funerals. It's a small orchard with a collection of well-tended apple trees.

Fyodor bends down and pulls up some weeds by their roots, tossing them aside.

"They choke the growth of the saplings," he says. "We plant them to celebrate new life. The tree for your *malyshka* is right here."

A slender young apple tree leans against the wall, its roots carefully packed in plastic.

Dani prepares the sapling. I pick up a shovel and start digging.

"Can I do it?" Vera is reaching for the shovel.

"Of course."

Vera makes short work of it, and within a couple of minutes, the hole is plenty big enough.

Dani and I put the tree in place, holding it straight as everyone takes turns packing a handful of soil. I pat down the last of the earth, and the new sapling is planted.

"New beginnings," Dani says. "For all of us."

No one speaks for a minute. I look around at the cycle of life - trees young and old, headstones here and there. The ground is littered with crispy leaves, a carpet of gold and bronze. One largish tree is at the end of its productive phase, and the fruit lies rotting on the ground below it.

A small sign at the base of the tree gets my attention. Leaves partly obscure it, and I brush them away with my boot. The writing is still clear.

For Mikhail.

"We planted this for you when Erik and Idina took you away," Marta says. She puts her hand on the tree's trunk. "You were just a baby. We loved you then, and we love you now. Your blood, our blood - it's meaningless, Kal. You're one of us."

Dani takes my hand. I pull her close, and she nestles her head into my chest.

Something occurs to me.

"Fyodor, you said *malyshka*. You think our baby is a girl?"

"I hope so." Fyodor's face splits into a broad grin. "I love having daughters. Imagine the fun I'll have with a little *dorogaya* around!"

Dani laughs. "At least you can do your faces-in-food thing for a bit longer!"

∼

"I'm glad today is over," I say as Dani unlocks the door to her home. "Maybe Vera and I will feel differently now that we've got some closure."

"It'll take time." She smiles at me. "You need to be kind to yourself."

Dani looks around and sees Pippa's purse.

"Oh, thank goodness we're not too late," she says. She shouts into the apartment. "Pip!"

Pippa runs out of her room wearing a towel, strands of wet hair flicking out behind her. She shrieks when she sees me, retreating out of sight.

"Dani! Kal nearly saw my boobs!"

I laugh. "Pippa, my fiancée is pregnant. Her boobs are ginormous right now. I don't need to look elsewhere."

I hear her snort. "Mine are still bigger. Not that anyone benefits from me having fabulous—"

"Stop it, Pip!" Dani giggles as she goes into Pippa's room. A moment later, they both emerge, Pippa wrapped in a robe.

"You're so late," Dani says, pointing at the wall clock. "You should have been at JFK an hour ago. Who are you, me?"

"I can get a later flight if I have to. There are so many to Moscow."

"I can't believe you got an interview," Dani says. "I'll be super excited for you if you get in. The Baikal Institute is so mysterious. You could write a book."

"I could, but I have to get a foot through the door first."

I didn't know Pippa was going there. I heard some things about that place when I was in the *Spetsnaz*, but it doesn't seem like a good time to get into that.

"So anyway, you two are getting under my feet," Pippa says. She's carrying a Coke in one hand and a toaster waffle in the other, trying to pick up a pair of jeans from the clean laundry pile with her foot. "So scooch. I'll shout up when I'm going."

Dani and I climb the stairs to the attic space. It's crammed with canvases; some finished, some barely started. She gestures at the one by the window.

A deep burgundy reaches across from the left, meeting the bright silver in the middle. The silver paint is layered thickly over the darker color, and where they mix, a pale, fresh lilac.

"I never realized before," Dani says, smiling, "but after we met was when the darker colors began to dominate. When all my work was destroyed, the new pieces were darker than ever, but they brightened over time. See?"

I look around the room. She's right. Her works from a few weeks ago are deep jewel shades of purples and indigos, but the more recent ones have more and more light creeping in. Some have pieces of mirror sprinkled across the canvas, making it seem like the light is moving through the darkness, conquering it.

Dani touches my arm. "It's all about us. The whole exhibition is about you and me. But don't tell anybody. Half the fun is making shit up when art journalists interview me."

"What will you tell them instead?" I say, kissing her forehead.

"Maybe I'll make up some nonsense about the irrepressible march of time and the turning of the planet bringing the nights and days. I don't know. I'll do it on the night."

"Speaking of which, when are you hoping to hold the exhibition?"

Dani shrugs. "After the baby is born. There's no hurry, and I want to give it my full attention. And more importantly, have a drink. I'm not laying on tons of free alcohol and sipping a goddamn apple juice all night."

Pippa's voice. "Byeeee!" she yells. "I'll let you know how it goes. Try to behave!"

"Bye, Pip!" Dani shouts back.

The front door slams.

"I have no intention of behaving," I say, rubbing my fingertip over Dani's lower lip. "What would get you going right now, *milaya*?"

Dani bites my finger, and I laugh.

"What I want," she says, leaning close to my ear, "is a Quattro Formaggio with olives and pineapple."

I frown. "I'm not ordering that, Dani. People will think I'm a complete deviant."

"You'd better be joking. You wanna face my hormonal wrath?" She raises her fists to me. "I tagged you once, Antonov. Don't think I won't do it again."

"Terrifying," I say, heading for the stairs. "I'll go. But you'll pay for having the nerve to give me orders."

Dani grins.

"Don't threaten me with a good time!" she laughs.

EPILOGUE
DANI

Christmas Eve...

"Dani, you're late! You'll have to run for it, or you'll never make it on time!"

Mel is yelling at me from the hallway. She's trying to appease an irritable Brutus, who has been waiting outside in Papa's limo, engine running, for twenty minutes.

I slide up the zipper at the side of my dress and slip my tiara into place.

"Ready!"

Mama is behind me, gathering the flowers. She gasps as I turn around, her hand over her mouth.

"Oh, my Dani. You look beautiful." She fans herself with her hand. "I can't cry. I've no time to re-do my makeup."

Mama picks up my bouquet. "I'll take these to your father. He wants to be the one to hold them for you. And he needs something to keep his hands busy because he's been knocking back shots for the last hour."

I groan. Papa is a competent drunk, but I can't rule out the possibility of him falling on his ass while walking me down the aisle.

"Isn't he supposed to be taking it easy?"

Mama is on her way out the door. "You try and tell him that," she says. "He made more fuss when he had an ingrown toenail. Being shot in the shoulder is just a minor inconvenience."

I smile to myself as I hear my father wolf-whistling at Mama and her admonishing him for his cheek. If Kal and I are even half as happy as my parents, I'll consider that a win.

Pippa is back from Russia, and she and Vera are at my apartment with Kal. They make a good team, so I know Kal will be there in shined-up shoes and with his boutonniere on the right side. He doesn't mind his solitude, but I couldn't imagine him being alone on the morning of his wedding.

It was challenging to get him to agree to be away from me overnight. Ever since Idina attacked me, he's stayed by my side, and it's only recently that he's loosening up a little. It helps that I'm over the morning sickness and eating properly, and he's still doing all he can to take care of me.

My parents are already in the car. I run down the stairs and out the door, Mel hurling herself into the limo behind me.

Papa sighs when he sees me. "*Dorogaya*, I'm so proud. What a vision you are." He taps his watch. "But what time do you call this?"

Depraved Royals 241

I shrug, and he rolls his eyes, handing me the flowers.

"The roads are gonna be awful," Brutus says from the driver's seat. "So it's a good job you worked so much free time into your schedule."

"Less sarcasm and more driving," I say.

The snow is settling over the city. As we pass the south side of Central Park, it looks like the whole thing is tucked up under a soft white blanket.

The last time I saw snow like this, I was running late too. But I was trying to get away from Kal Antonov.

Now I'm running toward him.

Kal has had a lot to process since his mother died. With every week and month that passes, he's ever more optimistic, and now that my belly is swelling, everything feels more real to him.

With that comes fear. He wants to be a good husband and father, but Idina's voice still rings in his head, telling him he's no good. A lifetime of psychological abuse cannot be undone just like that; it takes time and care.

I'm up to the task because I love him.

I love every scar and every wound, be they physical or mental. I can't hate his struggles because they make him who he is. Instead of fighting the darkness, I encourage him to accept it as part of his personality's complex tapestry.

My family is a help. Papa is there to guide him, and Mama is gentle and understanding. Kal is beginning to realize that he doesn't have to let Idina live in his head, and Vera is getting there too. She's living with Mel, and they're becoming good friends.

The lights reflect on the wet sidewalk. The streets are packed with people getting their last-minute shopping done, meeting their family and friends, and making merry. So many happy people.

I look at my family sitting beside me. Mel is trying to tie a corsage around Mama's wrist, but she's struggling to make a neat bow.

"Melania, you are terrible at this," Mama laughs. "You spent years styling those dolls of yours, and you can't tie this properly?"

"Mama, it's been at least fifteen years since I last did that!"

"I used to braid your hair for you," Papa says. "Let me try."

All three break into giggles as my father inevitably does an even worse job.

"Perfect!" he cries. "Look at that, Dani!"

I smile.

On Christmas Eve, surrounded by the joy of the season, I might be the happiest person in the world.

~

The chapel is small. With so few in attendance, we didn't need much space.

A Bratva wedding is typically a big affair, but that's because most of them aren't proper weddings at all. Deals are brokered behind closed doors as the couple goes through the motions, trying to remember their duty.

Not so for Kal and me. We're marrying for love, and that's the beginning and end of the matter.

The news caused more than a few raised eyebrows, sure.

Danica Pushkin is marrying *who*? You're kidding. What's the scam?

Many people who move in criminal circles are still totally confused and waiting for the real story. It's hard for them to grasp that we're for real.

The string quartet starts up just as I'm shaking my skirts out. Pippa is at my side, helping Mel to arrange my train as Mama runs inside.

"This wedding is just like you two," Pippa says, fussing at my veil. "Crazy."

"Is Kal mad at me?" I ask. "I hope not. It's kinda his fault I'm late—"

Pip covers her ears with her hands.

"I don't wanna know. From what you've told me, it's gonna be something pervy, and I struggle to look him in the eye as it is!"

My Papa takes my arm. Pippa looks us over.

"Aww. Righto, I'm off. See you in about thirty seconds," she points, "right down there."

Pippa walks down the aisle beside Mel. They look so calm; you'd never guess they were frantically smoothing out my dress only seconds ago.

I squint. What's that?

The zipper on Pippa's dress has split from the bottom. It's not open all the way, but her panties are clearly visible. She takes her place at the altar beside Vera, who notices and moves to stand behind her.

I suppress a giggle and relax my face. *Time to go.*

Kal is watching me as I walk toward him. His eyes shine in the candlelight, and I remember the last thing he said to me before he left yesterday. He sees me blushing and smiles, knowing what I'm thinking.

My father takes my hand and puts it into Kal's.

"It's tradition," Papa says, "but I'm not giving Dani away, and you're not taking her." He kisses my forehead. "My girl gives *herself*."

The ceremony passes in a blur of repeated words and solemn promises. We exchange rings, and with that, the legal stuff is done.

"Before God and this congregation of love, I'm delighted to pronounce you man and wife." The priest nods at Kal. "You may kiss your bride."

Kal touches my bump with the back of his hand, stroking it gently before putting both hands on my waist. He pulls me close and lowers his lips to mine.

"Did you do what I told you?" he whispers.

"Yes."

Kal kisses me again, and my sister can no longer contain herself. She's brandishing confetti, throwing it over us.

"Wooooooo!"

"Mel, you're supposed to wait until we're leaving!" I laugh, brushing rose petals off my shoulders.

Papa shakes Kal's hand. "She's your problem now, kid. Hope you can handle her."

Pippa opens her mouth to say something, but I'm sure it's not gonna be anything my darling Papa wants to hear...

"Pip, your ass is hanging out," I say.

She reaches behind her and realizes what I'm talking about. "Oh, bloody hell. Never mind." She shrugs at the priest. "Aw, come on. Don't act like you don't want a look."

Everyone heads out of the church ahead of us, and Kal and I are alone for a minute.

"We don't have time to...you know," I say.

"It'll wait," Kal replies, kissing my ear, "but not for long. I was just thinking about Christmas. It's gonna be associated with very different things now."

"I guess the bad stuff from the past can be pushed out by all the good that's yet to come." I take his hand. "But for now, let's just have today to keep in our hearts. Every day of happiness is a gift."

"That's why they call it the present, right?"

I smile. "Right."

We walk out to a flurry of confetti and rice, running past my family as they cheer. Our wedding car is waiting, but I see no driver. As we reach it, Kal opens the passenger door, and I climb in.

"What are you...?"

"You'll see." Kal gets in and drives away, honking the horn as everyone waves goodbye.

I frown at him.

"Where are we going? I thought we were going for a meal."

It's alright, *milaya*. Everybody else is going to have food and live it up. But *we* are going on honeymoon."

"What, now?"

"Yep. Now stop asking questions."

After a short while of driving through the snow, the penny drops.

"We're going to the airport," I say. "Have you seen the weather? We won't be able to—"

"Not on a commercial flight, no," Kal grins. "Can you guess where I'm going with this?"

∽

Back on Kal's plane, this time in my wedding dress.

The world seems a different place compared to just a few months ago. Back then, he and I were worse than strangers. I hated him before I even met him. Now I can't imagine my life without him.

I recline on the seat as the pilot fires up the engine. The plane begins to move, slowly taxiing away from the terminal.

Kal is watching me as I massage my calf.

"I have a confession to make, Dani."

"Sounds ominous. What?"

"When I first met you, I had to lock myself in that bathroom," he says, pointing, "and jerk off just enough to not give myself away. You were driving me fucking wild."

"As much as I am now?" I smirk.

Kal and I have a piece of shared knowledge that we want to act on. But not while the seatbelt light is still lit.

"I'm only more crazy about you now. But that's not all." Kal takes a deep breath. "I got the pilot to lie about the weather being too bad to get to NYC. I just wanted to get you alone in London with me."

Sneaky bastard.

"To be honest, I guessed that part," I say. "It was sunny outside, and we were well out of Geneva. And it wasn't raining or foggy when we landed at Heathrow, either."

Kal laughs. "Trust me to try an excuse like that on one of the three days a year that the weather isn't shitty in London."

We take off, and within a few minutes, we're settled at a low cruising altitude.

The PA system lets fly with a burst of static before the pilot speaks.

"All good. I'm turning off the seatbelt signs now. Feel free to move around the cabin."

Kal pulls his seatbelt buckle, and he's out of his seat, kneeling in front of me. He leans in to kiss me, flinging my tiara across the cabin as he winds his hands through my hair.

"That was expensive," I murmur against his lips.

"I'll buy you ten."

He reaches for my skirt, trying to lift it. "Another outfit designed by some cock-blocking fucker. Help me out here. What do I do?"

I reach for the zipper at the side of the dress. Kal undoes my seatbelt so I can stand up, and I shimmy my hips, wiggling the dress down to the ground. I step out of it and kick it aside, with Kal still kneeling at my feet.

"Oh, I like you there," I say. "You look like you're worshipping me."

"I am."

As he instructed, I'm naked.

Almost.

He slides his hands up my legs, kneeling up to kiss my rounded stomach. "You're everything, Dani. There's nothing I wouldn't do for you."

Really? Well, husband — I have a question.

"Tell me what you wanted to do to me when you were jerking off in the bathroom."

Kal looks at me, a wide grin plastered across his handsome face.

"As luck would have it," he says, sliding his thumb over my pussy lips, "I wanted to turn you over, bend you over the back of this exact seat, and fuck you very hard."

"Be rude not to do it then, wouldn't it?" I turn away from his as I speak, bending slightly at the waist so he can see the evidence of my obedience.

"Holy shit," Kal whispers. He strokes my ass with his hand. "That's the hottest thing I've ever seen."

Nestled between my buttocks is a beautiful glass butt plug. It's a tear-drop shape, and at the flared end is a crown decorated with multicolored jewels.

I inserted it before I put on my wedding dress. Throughout the ceremony and ever since, it's been in my asshole, teasing my nerve endings and giving me tingles of pleasure every time I move.

Kal told me to do it, so I did. And now he knows I'll always play his filthy little games.

The hours of stimulation have got my pussy seriously worked up. I can feel my juice running down my legs, and as I bend over and open myself up, the empty feeling intensifies.

I want my new husband to rail me right here, but I don't need to say so. Because he knows, and he's gonna do it.

"Kneel on the seat," Kal says. His voice is thick with lust. "I wanna enjoy the view for a moment."

As I get into position, I hold the back of the seat for balance. I hear Kal undo his zipper, and he moans as he grips his cock, stroking it as he looks at me.

"This was what I imagined. Only it's better. That plug makes you look like such a slut." He takes a step, and I feel his warmth as he leans against my ass. Without warning, he slaps the plug's base, and I cry out.

"That's the good stuff," Kal murmurs, rubbing the head of his cock against my wetness. He slips between my pussy lips, stretching me open, and I arch my back as he fills me.

God, he feels good. I've wanted this all day.

Kal nudges the plug again, growling as my pussy clenches in response. He grips the flesh of my ass as he thrusts harder.

"D'you know what?" he says, slapping my ass, "I'm gonna fuck your ass. When I say so, relax and breathe out. Ready?"

I inhale deeply.

"Now."

I let out my breath and let my internal muscles go limp. The butt plug slides out easily with one firm pull from Kal, and he drops it beside the seat.

He slides his cock out of me, and I never felt more empty.

"Please, Kal. Put something *somewhere*! I'm too turned on to care."

Kal rests his slick cock in the valley between my buttocks, moving his length against my skin. He uses his thumb to pick up my natural lubrication and apply it to my tender asshole, getting it good and slippery.

"You want me in here?" He rests the bulbous head against me, pushing gently. "You want me to wreck your asshole? Because I'm not gonna go easy on you."

I push my hips back against him, so he slips into me a little more.

"You'd better mean that," I groan. "Fuck my ass. I wanna feel you come in there."

Kal takes hold of my ass cheeks in his hands and leans his weight onto me, nudging his cock past the tight ring of muscle. I wince as he fills me, my pussy spasming and clutching at nothing. My hand moves beneath me, reaching for my clit, and I'm astonished to find I'm so wet it's like a running faucet.

I brace my arms against the seat, biting my lip as Kal pulls almost all the way out of my ass before plunging deep inside again. It hurts, but the searing pain is jumbled up. My fingers are generating intense pleasure in my clit, and as it mingles with the stretching fullness in my ass, the overall feeling is indescribable.

My climax is taking hold when Kal's hand reaches around me, taking hold of my throat. He pulls me back and snarls as he picks up pace, slamming in and out of me faster and faster.

"You fucking dirty bitch," he says as he pounds me. "I never knew you were such an ass slut. You like all your holes ruined, don't you?"

I'm coming. How could I not? The man who loves me and wants to fuck me until I come screaming is one and the same. Could I be any luckier?

I scream and tense up, my muscles clamping onto Kal's cock, and he slams into me one last time, coming deep inside my ass. He collapses onto me, and I can hear him panting in my ear.

Kal pulls out of me and rearranges his clothing. I turn around in the seat and sit down awkwardly, aware that I'm probably getting his ejaculate all over the place.

He laughs when he looks up at me.

"Here," he says, rummaging in the carry-on luggage, "There's your maternity nightgown thing here." He passes it to me, and I slip it over my head, grateful to be covered up.

"Tell me this isn't all you brought, Kal. I need some actual clothes."

"When will you learn?" Kal sits in his seat and closes his eyes. "Of course I packed properly. There needs to be more trust in this marriage."

I smile. "I *do* trust you. With my life. And my heart. Just not with my luggage."

"Oh well," Kal says, yawning. "Two out of three is pretty good. And since you didn't ask, we're going to Paris."

I squeal with delight. "Paris? For Christmas?"

"Yes, and for all of January. You wanted to attend that lecture course, didn't you?"

"Thank you. What will you do while I'm studying?"

Kal shrugs. "I don't know. Maybe I'll just join a bohemian commune and sit around, brooding over whimsical poetry."

I watch him as he settles down to rest.

My husband. Kal Antonov - the man who earned the love of a princess and will become a king.

"You were right when you said we're royalty, you know."

Kal opens one eye.

"Nah, *milaya*. I'm a fucking pauper and always will be. But you? You're a queen. I love you, Dani."

I smile. "I love you too."

EPILOGUE
DANI

Dani's birthday...

"Are you *sure* Vera doesn't mind?" I ask yet again.

Kal sighs. He knows I fret, and he's trying to be patient.

"I told you, she's fine. You saw how she was practically kicking us out the door. We deserve this break, and Tiana loves her Auntie V."

I smile. He's right, of course. Our baby girl is five months old and is the most independent little creature ever. Far from clinging to me, she's out for adventure, already rolling and trying to head off into the world.

"I know, I just worry," I say, taking Kal's hand. "Don't think I don't appreciate this, though. Florence has always been a dream destination for me. But I wish you'd tell me why we're here."

"An exhibition, like I said. It's your birthday, and you know how I like to keep you guessing."

I'm distracted by the grandeur of the Palazzo Vecchio, standing above us in all its fortified glory. I never thought I'd see it in person.

The streets are calm and narrow, so unlike home. It's late, and there aren't many people around, but the restaurants and cafés still have a few lingering patrons enjoying their digestifs after a good meal.

"It's so beautiful here," I say. "The whole place is steeped in art and history. If I could, I'd spend years here just getting to know all the incredible people who came to define this city in Renaissance times."

"Hmmm," Kal says. "You know they're all dead, right?"

"No, they're not. They live forever in their deeds, just as we all do. Look here," I point as we round a corner onto the Piazza della Signoria, "do you know what this building is?"

"As a matter of fact, I do." Kal lets go of my hand and slips down a dark alley to a rear door. I scurry behind him.

"What are you doing?" I hiss. "We're not meant to be here! This is the fucking Uffizi gallery!"

"Did they rename it? I'm sure the name wasn't always so sweary. Are all the weird fornicating statues in here now?"

I try not to laugh, but I can't help it. "Seriously, what are you up to?"

"I said we were going to see a special exhibit, didn't I? Now shush."

Kal turns the door handle, and everything inside is darkness. He grabs my arm, pulls me inside, and closes the door behind him.

"Kal, I love you, but I swear to God if you've broken in here—"

All the lights come on at once. I can't see a thing for a moment, and I blink stupidly in shock.

"*Surprise!*"

The courtyard is full of people. Friends of ours from New York. Art agents, promoters, dealers, and the many friends I made while studying and teaching in Paris.

And best of all, my family.

"Papa! Mama!" I cry, flinging my arms around them. "Where's Mel?"

"Over there," Mama says with a nod, "trying to get that tall hunk of Italian stallion's phone number."

I see my sister looking hot in a satin evening dress. She's charming a tall man with jet-black hair and pecs for days.

"Woah." I raise my eyebrows. "Good for her."

Kal narrows his eyes at me. "Watch it, wife. I don't have a sense of humor about things like that, you know."

I smile mischievously and ignore him, turning to Papa.

"Why are you here?"

"To celebrate, *dorogaya*."

Papa flags down a passing server, handing me and Kal glasses of champagne. I catch his eye, and he wrinkles his nose. I suppress a smirk and dutifully sip the fizz.

"What, my birthday?" I ask. "It's wonderful you're here, but I don't get it."

Kal grins. Mama nudges him.

"You are *such* a pain in the ass, Kal. How could you keep this from Dani?" Mama turns to me. "You really don't know?"

I look around—canapés on silver trays, flutes of sparkling wine. People are leaning on the gallery's iconic pillars, chatting and laughing.

One door to the inside is open, a velvet rope blocking the way. Brutus is guarding it.

"Is that the secret exhibit?" I ask.

Kal nods. "Do you wanna go take a look?"

"Sure. But you and I should go in on our own first."

Brutus's stoic expression makes me giggle. I poke him in the stomach.

"Hey, big guy. You been on the pasta or what?"

Brutus tries, but he can't keep the smirk off his face. "Hiya, Dani. Happy birthday, kid."

"Thanks," I say. "Let us in?"

Brutus unclips the rope and holds it aside.

"You got ten minutes," he says, winking at Kal.

Inside the room, the lights are low. Kal finds a switch on the wall and slowly turns up the dimmer, illuminating the art on the walls.

It's mine.

My debut collection is on display in the Uffizi Gallery, one of the most prestigious exhibition spaces in the world.

I'm staring. This can't be real, surely.

I turn to Kal. "How did…I mean, you…what?"

Kal laughs and pulls me into his arms. "What, this? I just flew Pippa here to take over the placement of your artwork that I had specially packaged and couriered from your home to Florence on a chartered flight. Anyone having an exhibition in New York in the next couple of days will find that everyone on the scene is mysteriously out of town—I told absolutely everyone to be here and bought out a couple of flights in their entirety to make it happen."

I look up at him, amazed.

He's always doing shit like this. When I went into labor, I had an entire suite of rooms and a private obstetrics team, most of whom played Canasta with me for hours because they had nothing to do.

"It's wonderful," I whisper, my eyes spilling over. "This might be the best thing you've done for me yet."

Kal glances at his watch.

"Give it a bit longer before you decide," he says. "In the meantime, we have a few minutes of solitude, and I have a great idea. Follow me."

He leads me past my art exhibition and to the back of the room, where another door leads to a flight of stairs. We emerge onto a balcony overlooking my surprise party.

I'm about to wave and shout to my parents when Kal grabs me around my waist, clapping his hand over my mouth.

"Shh," he hisses in my ear. "Don't make a sound." His hand reaches for the hem of my cocktail dress, pulling it up over my hips. "I want to fuck you here, where anyone could see if they look up. They won't be able to see what we're actually doing, but it's probably not wise to get anyone's attention."

Kal's fingertips slip under the elastic of my panties, dragging them down my thighs. I can't get my legs very far apart, but he doesn't seem to mind.

"If I just slip inside you, can you keep it together?" he asks. I feel him undoing his zipper, and then his cock is against my ass, hot and throbbing.

I nod, and he removes his hand from my mouth.

"That's my good girl," he murmurs. "Lean over a little, hands out. I won't fuck you too hard."

Yeah, right, I've heard that before. My husband likes to make love to me, but he likes to fuck me even more.

I sigh as he presses the tip of his cock against my pussy. Just the lightest touch is enough to trigger a gush of wetness, and he moans as he slips inside me.

"I'll never get used to how good you feel," he says. He holds my hips, withdrawing from me only to shove his cock back inside roughly. "No, no," he mutters, "I said I'd go slow, and I will."

I grind my pussy onto him, and he growls in my ear.

"Oh, it's like that, huh?" He gives me another firm thrust, sending a bolt of pleasure through my core. "I'd better even the odds a bit."

Kal reaches for my clit, finding the swollen little bud quickly. I bite my lip, suppressing a cry as his fingertips slip over it, jangling my nerves and making my pussy clench involuntarily.

"Holy shit, Dani. You keep doing that, and this will be over pretty fucking quickly."

I bump my ass into him, slamming his cock inside me to the hilt.

"So get on with it," I say. "You're all talk, Antonov. Where's the action?"

I know what I'll get for that kind of wise talk, and Kal doesn't disappoint. He rubs my clit more insistently as his thrusts pick up pace.

"You want *action*?" he gasps, biting my earlobe. "You need to come in silence, Dani, and I don't think you can, but I love you enough to help."

He puts his hand over my mouth again, the other still touching my clit. The restraint and control are enough to push me over the edge, and I scream into his palm as my climax wracks my body. My wet pussy spasming on his cock is too much for Kal, and he lets out a long, low moan as he fills me with his come.

No one looks up. I don't think anyone even saw us up here, let alone what we just did.

Kal pulls away and zips up, pulling up my panties for me as he does so.

"I think you need a bathroom, *milaya*. You're full of my come, and as much as that does it for me, you might not want to receive your guests in such a slutty state."

"You're incorrigible," I say, smiling. I remember something I meant to ask. "Is Pippa still here?"

"No. She had to go back to Moscow today, but she'll be back next week to visit."

I frown. "Kal, we can't do that. I can't be away from Tiana for that long!"

Kal looks past me and out onto the courtyard.

"It's funny you should say that..." his voice tails off, and I turn to see what he's looking at.

Vera walks through the door into the courtyard. My baby daughter is in her arms, looking adorable in a linen romper and bonnet.

I can't get down the stairs fast enough. I dash past Kal, almost tripping over my feet as I run across the courtyard.

"Tiana, my beautiful girl!" I cry.

My baby hears my voice and twists around in Vera's arms, looking for me. Her chubby little face lights up when she sees me reaching for her.

Vera laughs as I scoop Tiana toward me, nestling her against my chest. She coos and grabs my necklace, putting the pendant in her mouth.

"Hiya Dani," Vera says. "Guess you weren't expecting us!"

I look back to see Kal walking toward me.

That asshole husband of mine fucked me when he knew Vera would turn up any minute with the baby. I'll get him for that...

Kal is at my side. Tiana is resting her head on me, looking away, and hasn't noticed him yet. He leans close to her ear and blows gently.

"Hey, *malen'kaya printsessa*," he says gently.

Tiana whips her head around at the sound of her father's voice, letting out a squeal of delight. She reaches for him, her star-shaped baby hands grasping eagerly at his shirt. He laughs as he takes her from my arms.

"We're staying a while," Kal says to me. "Pippa will be back to help you do press and promotion stuff for the exhibition, and Vera is gonna hang around to help with Tiana."

Vera shrugs. "Meh. I get to hang out with my lovely sister-in-law *and* look after this little munchkin." Vera tweaks Tiana's toe and is rewarded with a high-pitched giggle. "I mean, how it that even work?"

We find my parents, and as she always does when Tiana is around, Mama loses the power of coherent speech.

"My wickle schweetie baba..." she says, booping Tiana's nose.

"Marta," Papa says sternly. "Words in English, please."

She raises an eyebrow. "You called her your pumpkin-y wumpkin-y the other day, Fyodor, so I'm not having that from you."

Papa frowns, then shrugs. "It's a fair cop. Can we go into the exhibition yet?"

Brutus is moving the rope aside, and the guests are filing in, grabbing more champagne as they go.

"Go for it," I say. "We'll be right there."

We watch as everyone goes inside, Mel arm in arm with her companion. Mama turns to give a little wave as she and Papa go inside.

Kal, Tiana, and I are alone for a minute, enjoying the cool evening air. Kal cradles our daughter in his arms as she dozes against his shoulder.

"You know what?" I ask as he wraps his other arm around me. "I never cease to be amazed by you. You're the best husband and father I could ever ask for. I love you."

I look up at him to see his smile break into a chuckle.

"Yeah, maybe," he says. "But we just had sex on the balcony. And I had to bribe *and* threaten the curator of the Uffizi to get you this exhibition space. So I'm still not the best guy."

I shrug. "No. You're the worst best guy ever. But I wouldn't change a thing."

"Me neither, *milaya*. I love you." He drops a kiss onto Tiana's sleeping forehead. "And you too, tiny human."

The stars are coming out. We enjoy a minute of peace before Mel's head appears around the door.

"Come on, Dani!" she cries. "Time to shine, girl!"

Kal drapes his arm over my shoulder as we walk over.

"There's never a time you *don't* shine," he says, "but this is *your* moment. I'm so fucking proud of you, do you know that?"

I nod, trying to suppress the tears.

"Good. I'm gonna hang back for a minute. Go be amazing."

I kiss him. "Thank you for doing this."

"Hey, I get to love you. The rest is easy."

MAILING LIST

Thanks for reading! Reviews are appreciated. I hope you enjoyed this book.

Want a FREE bonus chapter? Sign up to my mailing list and get it emailed straight to your inbox.

Sign up at this link:

https://dl.bookfunnel.com/n5celyg56k

ALSO BY CARA BIANCHI

Thanks for reading!

If you enjoyed **Depraved Royals**, you may also be interested in reading **Twisted Sinner**. It's a standalone story but's it's set in the same universe, with Kal, Dani and their family making a cameo appearance!

Twisted Sinner

Santori Mafia Kings

1 - Bound to the Devil

2 - Stolen by the Killer

Dark Russian Mafia Standalones

Tainted Vow